Best Friends Don't Leave

DEBBIE IHLER RASMUSSEN

M.O.M.M.
PUBLISHING

Mysteries of My Mind

For information contact:
authordebbieihlerrasmussen@gmail.com
Website: authordebbieihlerrasmussen.com

Published by:
M.O.M.M. Publishing
"Mysteries of My Mind"

Cover Design collaboration:
Dee Loupeti • www.deegraphicdesign.com and
Francine Platt • www.edengraphics.net
Cover photos: istockphoto.com – subman and LiuNian

Interior Design:
Francine Platt • www.edengraphics.net
Photos:
Bridge photo: Rue Ware
Lone Surfer: dreamstime.com – Epicstock

Editing:
Lisa Russo Leigh and Audra Wright

978-1-7334645-6-7 Paperback
978-1-7334645-7-4 ePub

Library of Congress Number: Pending

First Edition
Manufactured in the United States of America
10 9 8 7 6 5 4 3 2 1

Dedicated to
My wonderful friends near and far…
I treasure you.
I am blessed to have
too many to try to list here…
But you know who you are….

XOXO

SPECIAL THANKS TO:

At this point in my writing career, my special thanks is to MY READERS!!

Without readers, books are just words on pages and pages of paper.

I can't begin to tell ALL of you how much I appreciate your support, your encouragement, and honestly the love you share with me about my books.

It is because of many of you that these novella's from Mystic Trilogy are becoming a reality! You asked me to continue the Mystic story, so here we go!

I can't thank you enough for believing in me.

I hope we can continue this journey together for a very, very, long time.

Love, Debbie

Dear Readers,

I AM EXCITED to present to you the first in several 'back stories'
from *The Mystic Trilogy!*

So many have requested that the story continue—before I make
up my mind if that will happen, I decided it would be fun to take
a peek into the life stories of some of the characters in *Mystic Angel,*
Mystic Lake, and *Mystic Mansion.*

Their stories have always been in my head, that's where they are
created—but I am the only one who knows how they arrived at the
place when you meet them in the books.

We are starting with two of our main characters, Aspen and
Krista.

I hope you enjoy learning a little more about their history
together growing up in San Clemente, California.

Debbie

A good friend knows all your stories,
A best friend helped you write them.

PROLOGUE

JACKSON ALLEN rolled his truck to a stop and Aspen leaned against the back door. Her aching heart pounded inside her chest, but she kept her eyes fixed on her flipflops. Her parents, both sitting in the front seat of the truck, were silent, but she was sure her mom kept glancing at her. Her brother Noah, and his best friend Derrick Stanton, were having an indiscernible conversation on the other side of the truck. Every so often they would chuckle, but not laugho. Today was not about laughing.

Aspen glanced up and turned her eyes towards the front door of Krista's house. Krista Steele, Aspen's best friend since the two of them were four years old, had not emerged. Since she had not shown up at the Allen residence this morning at the appointed time, Aspen, Derrick and Noah walked the short distance to Krista's.

Maybe Krista thought if she didn't say goodbye, Aspen's leaving wasn't real.

Aspen sighed. But it was real.

Aspen sensed her dad's impatience, though he said nothing. She was aware of the long drive ahead. Dad had been in a perpetually bad mood since he announced the move. The thought of the strained silence for the past two months in their otherwise joyful home, caused more anxious feelings to well up inside her. Especially right now. She knew they could not wait much longer.

It had been two months since Dad announced they were moving from San Clemente, California to Sommerville, Tennessee… wherever that was.

Aspen and Krista had spent every waking, and even some not so waking, hours together. They had shed so many tears, Aspen was not sure she had any tears left. But her heart cried. So much it hurt to breathe.

The air was crisp on this early May morning and Aspen shivered. She pulled the hood of her sweatshirt a little tighter and resolved she'd have to go to Krista's door. She was not leaving without saying goodbye.

Suddenly the front door flew open.

"Aspen!" Krista wailed as she ran down the sidewalk and threw herself into Aspen's arms. "I hate that you're leaving! What am I going to do?"

Aspen pulled Krista into a tight hug and the two girls wept openly.

"I'm going to miss you so much." sobbed Aspen.

Krista choked on her own sobs, "Maybe you'll be back before school starts next year."

Aspen held her best friend at arms-length. "We have to be—I can't bear school without you!"

They hugged again and Aspen felt Krista's two little sisters hugging her legs.

Aspen bent down, hugging the two little, curly-headed blondes. It was then she heard Krista's mother and father, who were standing on either side of the truck, talking through the open windows to Jackson and Suzann Allen.

Krista gently moved her two sisters out of the way and threw her arms around Aspen again. They said nothing as sobs racked both of the girls bodies.

"C'mon, Aspen. We need to go." Noah gently tapped his sister's shoulder and when Aspen released Krista, Noah immediately pulled Krista into a tight hug. Derrick hugged Aspen and then the four stood in a small circle, saying nothing.

Finally, Noah reached for Derrick's hand. "Well bro, guess this is it."

Derrick ignored Noah's hand and pulled him into a hug. "Yeah." he choked.

Noah briskly wiped a tear from his cheek, half smiled at Derrick and walked deliberately around the back of the truck and climbed into the back seat.

Derrick wrapped his arms around both girls, but then stepped away and joined Krista's parents and sisters who had now moved to the sidewalk.

With swollen eyes and tear-stained faces, Aspen and Krista stared at each other for a few seconds. Aspen squeezed her friend's hands and then she quickly climbed into the back seat she would share with Noah on the long drive to Tennessee.

It was only five am, but the rising sun peeked through the clouds. No marine layer today. Weird.

Noah lifted one hand to wave at Krista and then he turned away. His sullen look expressed his exact attitude for the last two months, only now his eyes were filled with sadness.

Krista pushed the truck door shut and Aspen opened the window.

"Bye Krista. Bye Derrick." Her parents nearly said their names in unison. Mom leaned across the seat and waved to their friends through Dad's open window. Dad barely lifted his left hand acknowledging them and started the truck engine.

Derrick walked around the back of the truck. He pulled one hand from his shorts pocket for one more goodbye to Noah.

Noah returned the wave. Aspen was sure he would cry if he even tried to speak. He was leaving his best friend in the middle of his junior year in high school and he had not wasted any time letting his parents know how unhappy he was about it. But his disapproval did not change anything. The family was still moving.

Dad drove the truck away from the house and up the winding street. Aspen leaned out of the window waving until Krista's family, Krista, and Derrick, finally disappeared from her view when the truck rounded a corner.

She sank back into her seat and closed her eyes, uncontrollable sobs wrenching her chest. In her entire fifteen years she could never remember feeling so miserable.

In our beginning… (we were four)

"Want to come to my house?" I did not wait for Krista to answer. "I have a swing set!"

"Okay!"

Krista's mother followed us while we skipped down the sidewalk from Krista's new house to my backyard.

That's how immediate our connection was. At four years old, it was like we had known each other forever—well for four years. We were inseparable. Growing up together, we spent as much time at each other's houses as we did at our own.

Noah was a part of it too. It was always the three of us hanging out until Noah and Derrick met in the sixth grade, then our threesome became a foursome.

Derrick and his dad lived in a small beach house right across from the pier. We lived on the street right behind him, only up the hill and a few houses from Krista. Both Krista's and our house had a west wall of windows providing the most beautiful views of the ocean. Needless to say, we spent most of our time on the beach.

Derrick's dad, Dave Stanton, was a surfer and fit every description I had ever heard of a hippie from the sixties. Long blonde hair, deeply tanned, always in swimming trunks unless he was forced to put on a t-shirt; and in no hurry to do anything. After his wife died when Derrick was in elementary school, he sold his home on the hill and moved to the beach. He quit his job and started teaching surfing lessons; later partnering with a friend and they developed the Junior Lifeguard Program in San Clemente.

Dave was the same age as our parents and when they were all at the beach they seemed to be cut from the same cloth; but Dad ran a huge financial company. He wore shorts, t-shirts, and flipflops most of the time, too. Although, he did put on actual shoes, slacks, and a casual shirt when he had a business meeting. Mostly he was in flip flops. Even though he had long hair in most of the pictures, nearly to his shoulders, when Noah and I were little, he had long since cut it. Still, to his chin, it was longer than a typical hair length for a man in his forties.

Mom and Dad started Noah and me surfing when we were little—maybe when Noah was three and I was two, when we lived in Dana Point. When they built our house over-looking the beach in San Clemente, they had us in the ocean even before we moved in. I thought it was a normal life—to be in the ocean day in and day out. When I was in elementary school, I honestly didn't realize there were kids who didn't get to spend every day at the beach. Whenever we traveled it was always to a place where there was an ocean, so why wouldn't I think that?

Starting with kindergarten, Krista and I were in the same classes all through school. Something we carefully orchestrated. And it was no small feat! We had to beg teachers and counselors sometimes and other times we had to beg our mom's to do the begging for us, either way, the begging worked.

We had lots of other friends, too. It would take forever to name them all, but they were avid surfers like us, so we were a pretty tight group. But our foursome shared an unspoken bond all our own.

(we were seven)

Our mom's started us in ballet lessons. Neither of us were too excited about it, but we went willingly to class. We left willingly too! There we were all decked out in our pink leotards and pink tights, with our pink ballerina dance bags containing every little girls' coveted pink ballet slippers. Every little girl but Krista and me.

After about ten minutes at the barre, Krista whispered in my ear from behind me. "I'm going home."

I whispered back. "What?"

At that, Krista turned and walked out of the room with our startled ballet teacher, Miss Betsy, calling after her.

Well I for sure wasn't going to be stuck there alone, so I followed her. We both grabbed our tennis shoes and hurried out the front door. We ran almost two blocks in our pink ballet shoes, never to be worn outside mind you. We found some grass and quickly changed shoes. We flung our pink ballerina bags over our shoulders and started for home. Five miles!

We hadn't gone far when our very anxious mothers pulled up alongside us. Miss Betsy had called them to report we were AWOL from ballet class. They hurried to our rescue. It was not a pleasant day for us—what with leaving Miss Betsy freaking out because two seven-year-olds were out on the streets on her watch, and the near destruction of two perfectly good pairs of pink ballet slippers. Not to mention the three months of lessons our mothers paid for in advance. Nonrefundable. They paid the new student discount price.

Yeah, we both got to know the inside of our bedrooms—alone—for two whole days! Not fun, but hey, we didn't have to take ballet and as soon as we were ungrounded we were back at the beach. Our moms laughed about it later—after they took flowers and chocolates to poor Miss Betsy. We never did hear if Miss Betsy ever laughed. Probably not. She was quite serious about her ballet class!

By the way, the pink leotards were better used as swimsuits. Just sayin. I'm not sure what happened to the ballerina bags or the tights, or ballet shoes. They were, after all, pink.

(we were nine)

For Krista's ninth birthday, her aunt took Krista and me to the Wild Animal Park in Escondido. It was a hot Southern California day and in our hyperactive nine-year-old selves, we had literally dragged her aunt from one exhibit to the other. We were finally exhausted, and she decided to take us on the train. I guess she knew she would have us confined.

No sooner had the train started when we both fell asleep. Other than getting on the train, I only remember one thing. The train stopping suddenly. It woke both of us up.

We were rocking all over the place and Krista's aunt put an arm around each of us holding us tight. It was an earthquake! We had both been through earthquakes before, but this one was different. We weren't at home with our parents.

The animals were all running, and the conductor was calmly telling us it was just an earthquake.

Just an earthquake??

Wide-eyed, Krista and I stared at each other. The shaking stopped and tears welled up in both of our eyes. But not for long.

Krista's aunt suddenly said, "wow extra excitement we didn't know was included in the price of a train ride!"

We both laughed, and all was well again. But we talked about the scary earthquake forever!

That was the second time Krista had been with me when I saw a spirit.

The first time was in first grade on the playground. One day Sami showed up, and when I told Krista about my new friend she looked at me with wide eyes; but said nothing. Krista never talked about Sami. She never questioned me; even though Sami played right alongside of us. I suppose Krista was trying to figure out who the heck I was talking to.

But this time it was a girl about our age, on the train sitting on the seat behind us. I glanced back at the people the girl was sitting with. It must have been a brother and sister and their parents. They did not seem to notice the girl. I did. She smiled at me. I quickly turned around. While the rest of us were a little jolted by the earthquake, she seemed to be unscathed. When I looked back again, she was gone. I didn't say anything to Krista or her aunt, but Krista locked eyes with me. She had the familiar 'not again' look in her eyes. But just as with Sami, she said nothing.

And so, it went…This brief description of my friendship with Krista is not at all a composite of the eleven years we were best friends—but I am sharing with you some of the events and reasons such a strong friendship and love developed between us. Krista was a friend I trusted with my innermost secrets; she knew me. Everyone should have this kind of friend relationship at least once—I did not know it then, but I would be lucky enough to have it twice…

Good friends are like stars,

You don't always see them,

But you know they're always there.

1

SOMETIMES LIFE TAKES YOU TO UNEXPECTED PLACES

(we were twelve)

"HEY!" Krista ran up the sidewalk to the Allen's front door as Aspen threw it open.

'What's all the excitement?"

"We're going to Utah—my parents said you could go. Do you want to?"

"Why are you going to Utah?"

"My great grandmother lives there, and she is really sick. My grandparents are dead, so since my sisters have a dance recital coming up Mom wants my dad to go without them, and he wants me to go too so I asked if you can come! We have to fly to Salt Lake and then drive there because she lives about an hour and a half from Salt Lake."

Aspen could not help but laugh at the speed twelve-year-old Krista delivered her announcement. She grabbed Krista's arm. "Let's go find out!"

The flight from San Diego, California to Utah was about an hour and a half. Krista had been to Utah once, when she was three or four, so she couldn't remember much about the trip except the drive to Great Grandma's was long and boring,

When the plane landed in Salt Lake the girls were mesmerized by the impressive Wasatch Mountains. It was mid-July and the mountains still had skiffs of snow on the peaks.

Two hours later after they picked up the rental car and had lunch, they were on their way south to a little town called Orangeville. Aspen had heard of Orangevale, CA, but not Orangeville, Utah.

Jim Steele, Krista's dad, had always struck Aspen as kind of conservative. He worked at a bank and usually wore slacks and dress shirts and even a tie. He was always fun and nice to Aspen and Noah, but he didn't get involved in his kid's lives like Aspen's parents did. It was Krista's mother who was from San Clemente and she was the ocean lover. But this time he was totally different.

Wearing shorts, a tee shirt, and a baseball cap, he seemed more like her own dad. They laughed a lot on the drive to Orangeville while he related stories of visiting the small Utah community many times when he was a kid.

"Wait till you see the bridge—the coolest thing about Orangeville in my opinion. And I'll show you the river where I learned to swim."

"You learned to swim in a river?" Aspen's eyes widened.

"I did. And trust me it was cold!" Jim laughed.

They drove through a long canyon ending up in a small town called Castle Gate and then a bigger town called Price. They stopped there for a bathroom break and to get some drinks.

Krista's dad told them a story about Castle Gate. He said before they widened the road through Price Canyon, the mountain had two sheer rock formations on either side of the Price River that appeared to open like a giant gate as travelers approached the narrow section of the Canyon– which is why it was named Castle Gate. He explained that two railroad lines—the Denver and The

Rio Grande—both met there years ago, and it had the finest coal in the area. Jim told them that Castle Gate is now a ghost town mostly filled with mining equipment.

Aspen was fascinated with history and especially loved to learn about old ghost towns.

Krista did not share her enthusiasm and after her dad's story asked how much longer till they would get to her great grandma's.

Jim laughed. "About thirty minutes. Its' mostly desert but pay attention to the interesting mountain formations through here. They are unique to this area of the country."

Jim was right. The mountains were tall and flat on top. Jim told them lots of old westerns had been filmed here. Krista perked up and showed more interest when her dad told them many of the John Wayne movies were filmed in this region.

John Wayne movies was a love Krista shared with her dad. Long since dead, his movies lived on in the true form of the old west. One of Krista's favorite sayings of John Wayne was 'we're burnin daylight.'

They passed through a small town called Huntington that boasted the widest main street Aspen had ever seen.

"I'm told it was because the streets were designed to turn wagons being pulled by horses back then." Jim explained.

Krista shrugged and looked at Aspen. "Makes sense."

Neither of us could picture wagons and horses anyway, so the explanation was of little significance.

It wasn't long before they turned off the main highway onto another road at a sign announcing 'Orangeville' and an arrow pointing west.

As they drove into the town they came to another road and when Aspen looked to the left what she saw took her breath away.

"Oh my gosh!" Aspen leaned over the front seat to see more clearly through the front window. "That is the coolest thing ever!"

"I told you!" said Jim.

Krista was equally as enthusiastic. "I don't remember this bridge, Dad."

"You were only two or three when you came last time. I'm not surprised you don't remember."

The trestle bridge was one lane with a walking path along the west side. The trestles rose majestically above the road and framed the bridge in an open canopy of perfectly arranged steel beams and supports.

"Can we stop and walk across it?" asked Aspen.

Jim chuckled. He checked his rearview mirror and then pulled to the far-right side of the road and stopped.

Eagerly the two girls jumped out of the truck. They waited for Krista's dad to drive across the bridge and then they both hurried to the walking path.

"Whoa! The water is moving fast!" Aspen was fascinated with the river below them as the water rushed over boulders and swept logs along in the swift current.

They were both peering over the side when a truck entered the bridge causing it to shake. Both girls grasped the steel rail and they heard Jim laugh as he approached them from the other side of the bridge.

"Okay that was a little scary." said Krista.

"Yes, but it's normal for the bridge to shake when a car crosses it. It won't fall down." said Jim.

Krista rolled her eyes at her dad. "Good to know!"

"I have never seen anything like this. Do we have these kinds of bridges in California?" asked Aspen,

Jim shrugged. "I suspect we do. I have never looked into that." He continued. "Grandma lives up the street. Let's go see her and you girls can come back down here later if you want. We have a couple of days."

Krista's great grandmother's house was two streets away from the bridge and about ten houses up on the left side. The house was a white one-story frame house with spatters of marigolds and petunias around the perimeter of the lawn. The expansive front porch sported two rocking chairs and a porch swing. The porch and railing needed a fresh coat of paint but still looked sturdy and did not take away from the quaint charm of the house.

The three exited the truck and walked up a narrow cement walkway that was chipped and eroded in some places. When they reached the front door, Jim pulled the screen door open and knocked on the window in the door covered in a white lace curtain.

Jim didn't wait for an answer—he opened the door and called, "Kay!" as he entered the living room.

"Jim you made it!" called a woman's voice as she entered from an adjoining room. She threw her arms around Jim hugging him tightly. She suddenly turned her attention to the two girls. "This can't be Krista!"

Jim grinned, "Kay, this is Krista and her friend Aspen. Surprisingly good choosing the right girl since you haven't seen her in over ten years.

"Well, she looks just like you!" Kay warmly hugged Krista and then Aspen. "I was hoping to see your mom and little sisters but I'm so happy you two came!"

Jim explained, "Kay is my cousin. She has been here with Grandma for a couple of months. We need to find an assisted living home for Grandma."

"Which I am not going to!" Came a voice from another part of the house.

Jim and Kay laughed, and Kay said, "Come meet your great grandma."

Aspen had never met any of her great-grandparents, so she wasn't sure what to expect when she saw Krista's great grandma.

The woman was in bed wearing a flowery nightgown. She appeared tall but was very thin and her long thin grey hair was pulled back in a low ponytail.

When Jim stepped through the door she grinned, and her eyes twinkled. "Jimmy!" she leaned forward and extended her arms.

Jim bent down and gave her a quick squeeze then he sat on the edge of her bed. "How are you Grandma? Giving Kay trouble I see."

Grandma narrowed her eyes. "Well I don't want to leave my home. I am fine here by myself! You kids want to stick me in some home to die." She raised one eyebrow.

"Go ahead, deny it."

"Oh Grandma that's not what we want to do…"

Grandma interrupted Jim. "Oh fiddle—okay not to die. But stick me away is a true statement."

Kay laughed. "We go round and round about this."

Grandma eyed the two girls then she put one hand to the side of her mouth as if to whisper, "They don't think I notice, but I notice everything."

Aspen's eyes widened and she opened her mouth to say something but closed it quickly and turned to Krista, who played right along.

Krista leaned toward her great grandma. "Want us to break you out?" she whispered.

"Ah! A rescue!" Grandma clapped her hands together.

Jim stood. "Okay Grandma," he laughed. "Let's get you up." He pulled the covers back and extended both hands to grandma. She grasped onto them and pulled herself up swinging her legs over the side of the bed.

She glanced at the girls. "I could jog but I like to make them think they are important." She winked.

Jim put his arm across Grandma's back and guided her into the living room. He led her to a pale green rocker where she sat, then Jim covered her legs with a colorful crocheted afghan throw.

He turned to the girls smiled and rolled his eyes. "The girls want to check out the bridge, Grandma."

Grandma clasped her hands together. "Oh, the bridge! One of my favorite things in this town." She smirked. "Well the bridge and the trees."

Kay sat in a chair next to Grandma and pursed her lips. "Those trees…" she turned to Krista and Aspen and started to say something else, but Grandma held up her hand to stop Kay.

Krista and Aspen exchanged a quick glance. "What trees?" asked Krista.

Jim sighed and plopped down on the sofa. "Up by the mine. Well, up a little higher than the mine. They—well Grandma says, they are kind of magical."

"Not magical, Jim. Magic. There is a difference. She turned to the girls. "You can hear things in those trees."

Aspen shivered. "What do you mean, hear things.?"

"What mine?" Asked Krista.

Grandma leaned toward Aspen, "Voices. Barely discernible, but if you listen you can hear them." She turned to Krista, "the old coal mine, up the canyon a way." She nodded in Jim's direction. "The trees are *farther* up. "

Krista and Aspen both looked from Grandma, to Kay and then to Jim.

Krista's eyes widened. "Really?"

Kay nodded. "That's what she says."

"Wow, right up your alley." Krista lightly punched Aspen's arm.

Now it was time for everyone else to be confused, well, everyone it seemed, except Grandma. She lowered her head a little but looked up at Aspen through her eyelashes and smiled.

Krista suddenly stopped when she noticed the surprised looks on Aunt Kay and her dad's faces. She quickly back peddled and shrugged. "Nothing. It was nothing. It's a joke between Aspen and me."

Aspen glanced at her friend but made no comment.

Jim stood. "Let's go grab our bags."

Kay stood as well, "Good idea! I have lunch started."

The girls followed Jim out the door and Kay disappeared into the hallway.

Aspen glanced back. Grandma was still smiling and looking right at her.

2

SMALL TOWNS HAVE BIG SECRETS

After lunch, Jim, Kay, and Grandma decided to talk and see if they could come up with a plan everyone could agree on. Krista and Aspen elected to walk to the bridge.

Orangeville was a small, older town. The houses were set far apart with decent sized yards, some homes were brick, but most were wood. Most yards had grass, some didn't. But all were well kept, at least on this street. The paved roads were unusually wide, like the ones in the town of Huntington they had passed through on their way here.

"My dad told me my great grandma was a little eccentric, but I think she's cool." Said Krista.

"What is eccentric?"

Krista shrugged, "I don't know, strange maybe?"

"Maybe. But she's funny too! She does not want to move to a home, either."

Krista frowned. "I know and it makes me feel bad. But they are worried about her. Aunt Kay has to go back to work and she and Dad are the only kids left."

"She seems pretty healthy, and sharp as tack."

Krista laughed. "She is totally healthy! That's the problem—well not a problem—but you know what I mean. They don't know what to do. But she's ninety-seven years old."

Aspen stopped walking and turned to her friend. "Ninety-seven!"

"Yes! Now you see why they are worried."

Aspen started walking again. "Wow, I want to grow up to be like her."

Krista laughed. "Right?"

The girls turned the corner onto main street and the bridge came into view.

Aspen's heart jumped. She was surprised at how enamored she was with this steel structure. It wasn't a huge bridge, narrow enough the cars had to take turns to cross. But there was something about it.

The girls quickened their step and soon were standing on the walking path. There weren't too many cars in the sleepy town, they had only seen one cross the bridge, and that was yesterday. They leaned over the rail watching and listening to the roar of the rushing water below them.

"The water looks deep." Said Krista.

"And cold." Added Aspen. She looked up to where the river was coming from. For as far as could see it wound through banks decked with grass and trees. Some trees were growing right up out of the river. The torrent unmercifully tossed twigs, leaves and some logs, nearly everything in its' path. It was beautiful. She hadn't seen a river like this before, up close anyway. But she was also very aware of the strength and majesty of such a river. The ocean she and Krista were familiar with, but this? This was new for them both.

Suddenly Krista pulled on Aspen's arm. "Hey come here. I just remembered something." She walked back towards the street—when she reached the end of the path she looked both ways and then crossed the road to the other side of the bridge.

"What are we looking for?"

Krista crept through some big boulders and Aspen followed—the river was getting closer, and louder.

Krista pointed. "That."

The girls had to yell to hear each other over the roar of the river.

All Aspen could see was more bridge. "What are you pointing at?"

Krista edged a little further, inching her way closer to the bridge—and the water. The ground was flat where they stood, and sort of a path, but the steep embankment about three feet from them caused Aspen's heart to beat a little faster.

"Careful, Krista. Don't slip or you will be *in* the river."

Krista didn't hear her, or if she did, she did not respond. But she did grab onto a branch of a sturdy tree looming over them and hung on until she got where she wanted to be. Carefully, Aspen followed her lead.

"Okay look at the bottom of the bridge—on the side. See the cable, or whatever it's called."

Aspen could only see one cable. It looked to be maybe two inches in diameter—maybe not quite that big, and it spanned the entire length of the bridge.

Aspen nodded.

"Well, my dad told me stories about him and his friends crossing the bridge on a cable." Krista's eyes were wide with excitement.

Aspen twisted her mouth. "On the *outside* of the bridge, above the raging water, *no protection*—at all." She yelled, making sure she emphasized outside and no protection.

Krista shrugged. "Well, we would hold onto the other cables, and stuff."

"We?"

Krista nodded. "Yes! Let's do it."

Aspen turned to the river. Besides the two obvious facts it was rushing so fast and roaring so loud it was almost deafening—the spray was gradually drenching them. She surmised it was also deep, considering the size of boulders it was cascading around and over. And it was a stupid idea.

"My mother will kill me if I die." Said Aspen.

Krista said nothing. They stared at each other for a few seconds then burst into laughter.

"Okay let's…"

"Hey!" a man's voice above them stopped Krista. They both looked up.

There was a tall, grinning policeman standing on the road next the bridge. He motioned for them to come up.

Aspen and Krista exchanged a quick glance and then deliberately climbed through the boulders until they were back on the road.

"Did we break the law?" asked Aspen. She didn't have to yell to be heard now.

The policeman chuckled. "No, there is no law that says you can't go down by the river." He extended his hand. "I'm officer Bill."

The girls each shook his hand and introduced themselves, first names only. He wasn't wearing a hat and his head was bald. Still, he appeared to be about the same age as their parents.

"I haven't seen you two around here, and I know everyone who lives in this town. So, I was a little concerned for your safety. This is a treacherous river, and you don't want to fall in."

Aspen took a deep breath. "No, we don't.. We were just talking about walking…"

"Over the bridge!" blurted Krista. "On the road! Is, is that dangerous?"

Officer Bill's eyes narrowed and then he grinned. "Well assuming no cars are coming, but don't get caught on there. You would practically have to climb the sides so a car wouldn't hit you." He pointed to the other side of the bridge. "Hence, the path."

"Yeah, good point." Laughed Krista. "We, we were just wondering."

Okay, well don't try anything stupid. People have been killed in that river. I've known some folks who pulled some pretty stupid stunts."

Aspen glanced at the river. "Yeah, I'm sure they have." She mumbled.

Officer Bill was still talking. "So, obviously you girls are visiting?"

They both nodded but Krista responded. "Yes, my great grandma."

"Oh, what's her name?"

"Great-Grandma Steele. My dad's grandma."

"Minnie Steele! I have known her all my life. Wonderful lady."

Krista stammered, "Uh yeah, I guess. No one has ever told me her first name."

"I hear they are trying to move her into a home, she isn't too happy about it." Suddenly Officer Bill stopped. "Wait! You must be Jim's daughter, right?"

Krista looked surprised. "Right! You know my dad?"

"Know him? I went to school with him—till he moved up north that is. He moved away when we were twelve—then I moved and went to high school over in Sanpete County, then after I graduated from the police academy I moved back here. Never left again. I don't think your dad has ever visited before—at least not while I have been here."

"I think he has, and I know he did once, I was maybe four."

Officer Bill thought for a minute. "Hm, must have missed him." Then he laughed. "He's at your grandma's now?"

Krista nodded. "Yep, he and Aunt Kay are trying to decided what to do with her." She twisted her mouth and wrinkled her nose. "I—I guess that's how to say it."

Officer Bill chuckled. "Well, she will go kicking and screaming for sure."

The girls laughed and Aspen suddenly had a visual of Grandma Steele kicking and screaming. It did not seem far-fetched at all!

"I'm going over there right now." Said Officer Bill as he started to walk away. "Be seein' you two around, I'm sure."

"Hey, uh sir?" said Aspen.

Officer Bill looked back but kept walking toward his patrol car. "Yes ma'am?"

"Krista's grandma told us about some—trees?"

He stopped and turned around. His brow furrowed. "She did, did she?"

Aspen nodded. "Do you know…?

"I think you best steer clear of those trees little ladies." He stood still like he was waiting for an answer.

They both shrugged and Krista said, "Why?"

Officer Bill got a faraway look in his eyes. "Trust me."

With that he turned, went to his patrol car, started the engine, and made a U-turn in front of the bridge. He then turned on Great Grandma Steele's street.

Surprised by his reaction, the two watched him until they couldn't see his car any longer.

3

I HAVE NEVER SEEN DEAD PEOPLE

ASPEN AND KRISTA slept in sleeping bags on the living room floor. Aunt Kay put a foam pad under them, and the two fell asleep early.

Aspen woke to a breeze blowing on her face. She fumbled for her phone and checked the time. It was five am. The breeze was coming from an open window and the lace curtain, matching the one on the window of the front door, moved back and forth..

Why would anyone have lace curtains? You can see right through them.

She put her hands behind her head and tried to get comfortable, but sleep had left her. Wide awake, she quietly crawled out of her sleeping bag, picked up her phone and trying not to wake Krista, backed out the front door to sit on the porch. She softly closed the door and then turned around.

"Good morning."

Aspen clasped both hands over her mouth to suppress her scream.

Great Grandma Steele was sitting in one of the high-backed wooden rockers on the porch.

"Oh my gosh! You scared me to death!"

Grandma chuckled. "I can see that." She patted the arm of the rocker next to her. "Have a sit."

Grandma had an afghan over her legs, different from the one yesterday. Aspen picked up the one folded on the empty rocker, sat down and placed it on her lap. She ran her hand across the stitching. The afghans were worn, but still in almost perfect shape. "Did you make these?"

Grandma nodded. "Many, many years ago. Back when my fingers did what I told them to do." She held up her hands revealing crooked, bony fingers.

Funny, Aspen had not noticed before. She smiled. "They are beautiful. I don't have that kind of talent."

"You can always learn."

"Yeah."

"If you are willing to take the time." Grandma paused. "What do you like to do?" What are you good at?"

Aspen grinned. "Surfing. Krista and I surf."

"Ahh, yes. I do remember hearing about surfing. Well see, that is something I can't do—nor *want* to do." She clarified.

"You could learn." Aspen's eyes widened, but then she smiled. "Well could have—learned."

Grandma nodded. "Maybe in the next life."

Aspen pondered her comment for a few seconds. "So, you believe there is a next life. After this one?"

Grandma's eyes lit up. "Of course, I do. I know there is. Both of my children, my parents, and my Lamont are waiting there for me." She smiled it seemed to herself but then she looked at Aspen. "I have seen them. I think you know there is an afterlife, Aspen." Her face wore a more serious expression now.

"I have never seen anyone who has died."

"I believe you have." Grandma was not looking at her now. She had her elbows on the arms of the chair and her hands folded in front of her.

A chill ran through Aspen. She had seen people, but it never occurred to her they might be dead. That caused her to shiver, and she turned in Grandma's direction, who was looking right at Aspen.

"I spoke to the young man who does my yard. His name is Joey, and he will take you and Krista to the trees."

"What about these trees?"

"You need to go. I am so glad Krista brought you with her." She reached over and patted Aspen's hand. "Trust me." Her eyes twinkled. "Be careful on the bridge. But you will both be okay."

"How did you…?

The door opened. "Morning!" Jim stretched as he stepped onto the front porch.

"Good morning!" Grandma almost sang the words. "Come and sit in the swing. Kay will fix breakfast. I think she will if she hasn't run away yet."

Kay pushed open the door. "Not yet, but I'm considering it." She laughed and turned her attention to Jim. "How fun for you to see Bill yesterday."

"Yeah, what a pleasant surprise. I didn't realize he was still around here. It's been over thirty years." Jim turned to Aspen, "He told me about the bridge."

"What about it? We were just looking at it."

"I know my daughter better than that," he laughed. "And so, do you. You two are trouble."

Aspen blushed.

The phone rang from inside.

"I'll get it!" called Krista. In seconds she appeared on the porch. "It's someone named Joey?"

Kay looked quizzically at Grandma. "He doesn't come till Thursday."

Grandma nodded but did not respond to Kay instead she said to Krista, "Tell him to come anytime. These two scoundrels are going to look at *homes* today." She scoffed.

Jim raised his eyebrows.

Grandma noticed and said, "I asked Joey to take the girls on a tour—to the trees. Any objections?"

Jim shook his head. "No objections. If it's okay with you." He was addressing Krista.

She shrugged. "It's okay. Who is Joey?"

Bewildered, Aspen stood and followed Krista and Kay into the kitchen to help with breakfast.

Joey parked his red pickup truck in front of Grandma's house and jumped out. Tall and muscular, his reddish blonde hair spilled over his ears and touched the neck of his t-shirt. He wore jeans, cowboy boots, and a baseball cap. His arms and cheeks were dotted with freckles. Grandma had explained Joey was four years older than the two girls, so he had a driver's license.

He loped up the sidewalk and walked directly to Grandma. "Miss Minnie!" he greeted her with a quick hug.

"Joey, dear. Thank you for coming." She turned to Krista. This is Krista, my great granddaughter, and her friend Aspen. They are from California."

Joey grinned revealing a row of perfectly straight, beautiful white teeth. "I figured as much."

Both girls laughed. "Why did you figure that?" asked Krista.

"Tans. We don't get that tan here in Utah and especially down here."

"Good point." Said Krista and Aspen nodded.

"So, I guess we are going to the *treeeees*." Joey's exaggerated trees made the girls laugh.

"Guess so!" Krista picked up the cooler Aunt Kay had filled with sandwiches, snacks and water and trotted down the porch steps.

"You kids have a good time." Said Grandma. "I will be here waiting for the verdict from my grandchildren."

Krista glanced back at Grandma and waved, then followed Joey to the truck.

She's talking about my dad and my aunt." Said Krista.

"Yeah, I heard. They're trying to move her to a home."

Krista glanced over at Aspen who stepped off the porch. "Geez, does everyone know about Grandma?"

Joe laughed. "Ain't many secrets in a small town."

Aspen stopped on the sidewalk and turned back to Grandma. She was looking directly at Aspen, her eyes twinkling. She nodded her head curtly. "Have a good time." And she brushed at the air with her hand, motioning for them to leave.

Aspen smiled and climbed into the truck next to Krista. She was surprised it had a bench seat.

"Aspen?" Grandma called to her.

Aspen turned around.

"Listen."

Aspen nodded and closed the door.

"What was that all about?" asked Krista.

"I-I'll tell you later."

Joey started the truck and pulled out onto the road.

"You can tell her now." He said. "I know all about you."

Aspen glared at him and Krista looked from Joey to Aspen and back again.

Joey sighed. "Look, your Grandma has a sixth sense about these things. She thinks you," he was speaking to Aspen, "might have a connection or something. She honestly believes you will *hear* things up in the trees."

Krista's eyes widened. "Well, Aspen does…"

Aspen elbowed her friend and Krista scowled, but she stopped.

"And what if I don't—hear things?" said Aspen.

Joey shrugged. "Then I guess Miss Minnie is wrong. But I have to tell you, she rarely is."

Joey turned the truck the opposite direction from Main street.

"Where are we going? Isn't that the way out of town?" Krista motioned toward Main Street and the bridge.

He nodded. "That's one way. We're going the back way, past the cemetery."

Aspen sighed. *Perfect.*

They drove straight for about three blocks—at least they seemed like blocks. But they were much longer than in San Clemente. Then the road curved to the right went down a slight hill and up again. All around them were green fields. Some corn, most, Joey explained, were alfalfa.

Joey pointed to a road on the left, it was almost wide enough for two cars to pass each other. "There's the road to the cemetery." Shortly they came upon a narrow wooden bridge.

"Wait! This is the same river, right?" Krista leaned forward to see better. "Can we stop here?"

Joey nodded and then shook his head. He laughed. "Yes, same river. No, we can't stop. Miss Minnie made me promise not to stop here. It's the old swimming hole and she is sure your dad wants to show it to you."

Aspen's eyes widened. "Your dad learned to swim in *that* river?!"

They both looked at Joey.

"He did. We all did. The closest swimming pool is in Price and that's thirty miles away. And that," Joey laughed. "It's why we don't have tans!"

They drove a little farther then turned left onto a much wider road, with a white line dividing the two lanes.

"These mountains are so beautiful—and different." Said Aspen.

"Yeah, they remind me of the mountains in the western movies I watch with my dad." Said Krista.

"They probably are the same—or at least in the vicinity. These flat-topped mountains in Southern Utah were the location of a lot of westerns. Can't you just see the Indians lining up across the top before ambushing a wagon train?" Said Joey.

Krista laughed. "Actually, I was picturing that exact scene."

"Krista's dad loves western movies, especially John Wayne." Explained Aspen.

"A man after my own heart." Said Joey, and the two girls looked at each other and both raised their eyebrows.

The road ahead of them curved to the right and was surrounded on both sides by the flat-topped mountains. Aspen was excited to see them close up. To her disappointment, just before the road curved, Joey took a right turn onto another road that, again, like the ones in town, was not marked with lines.

"Dang, I was hoping we could go farther up the mountain." Said Aspen.

"Not today." Said Joey. "The treeeees are up here." He glanced over at Aspen and winked.

Aspen shivered. *What is that supposed to mean anyway?*

The paved road soon turned to dirt and Joey slowed down a little. The scenery was pretty. Wildflowers, grass, and trees were on both sides of the road. A few campers with either tents or motorhomes were partially hidden by the more dense clumps of trees.

Krista shrugged. "I don't see anything significant about these trees."

Aspen nodded in agreement but said nothing. The windows of the truck were open, and she was trying to listen.

As the truck rounded a bend in the road they spotted what looked like a gravestone a few feet to the right of the road.

"Who would put a headstone clear up here?" asked Krista.

"I guess if someone were buried here," said Joey, "but it's not a headstone. It's a monument some kids put here for their great grandma I think."

"What did she do?" asked Aspen.

Joey shrugged. "I don't know. Maybe just lived."

"Well, hey, we are living. We should have one of those too," said Krista.

Aspen laughed. "We will, it's called a headstone."

Krista wrinkled her nose. "Oh yeah, I guess it is."

The truck slowly crawled past more wildflowers, more clumps of trees and more campers. The road straightened out for a little distance but then took a long slow curve to the right and then to the left. As they came out of the last turn, both Aspen and Krista gasped.

The scenery suddenly turned to thick, skinny trees whose tall white trunks stretched majestically toward the sky.

Joey stopped the truck, but he did not turn the engine off. "These are Quaking Aspen's."

The narrow dirt road stretched almost straight before them and disappeared over the horizon.

Both Aspen and Krista's eyes widened.

"You're named after a tree!" said Krista.

"No, actually a city in Colorado."

Krista's eyes narrowed. "Really? You never told me that."

Aspen laughed. "I don't know, I saw a picture of Aspen, Colorado one time and it was so pretty so I decided my name came from there." She turned to Joey, "Are we at the top of the mountain?"

"At the top of this one, but if we kept going there are more mountains, the road goes into a valley first," said Joey.

"Have you been there?" asked Krista.

Joey nodded, "Many times."

"What's over there?"

Joey waved his arm out the window in a sweeping motion. "More trees." He put the truck in gear and rolled forward. When he came to a clearing on the side of the road he pulled over, stopped, and shut off the engine. "The odd thing about these trees is the leaves. Quaking Aspens are notorious for having sparse leaves about halfway up the trunk, with flourishing green at the top. If you notice, there are very few leaves on the lower parts of these trunks, and not even that many towards the top. It's weird."

Aspen nodded absently. The ground on the right side of the truck was flat and then gradually rose to a hill, completely covered in the leafless quaking aspen's. To the left, the ground rose about four feet straight up from the road and then nothing but trees.

She opened the door and climbed out and Joey did the same. Krista followed Aspen.

Joey walked to the back of the truck and let the tailgate down and then jumped up and sat on it.

Krista and Aspen just looked at him.

"I guess you're supposed to *listen*." He said and raised his eyebrows.

"Well, I'm glad Dad suggested we wore shoes and not flipflops. Should we walk up there?" Krista pointed to the side of the road slanting upwards.

Aspen shrugged. "Sure." And she followed her friend into the trees.

They walked for several minutes through thick grass in some spots and other places bare ground with only scattered leaves and twigs.

"Do you hear anything?" asked Krista.

Aspen laughed. "Nothing but the scrunching of our feet on these leaves. What am I supposed to hear anyway?"

"I don't know. Didn't Grandma tell you what to listen for?"

Aspen shook her head. "Nope."

They kept walking as the incline got steeper.

"If nothing else, it's really pretty up here," said Krista.

"Yeah, it is."

"Should we go over to the bridge later?"

Aspen's eyebrows furrowed. "Are we planning to scale the side?" she chuckled.

"I think we should."

"I'm sure you do." Aspen stopped walking. "I'm hungry, let's go eat lunch."

The girls turned and started back down the mountain.

"Have you ever been camping, Krista? You know, like in a tent?"

"Only at the beach, like you. Not in the mountains like this. Why?" "It might be fun."

"Or work. And what do people do up here? Just walk and hike?"

They were almost to the truck and Joey heard Krista's comment.

"We fish, and hunt and sometimes we listen to the quiet." Joey slid off the tailgate and pulled the cooler from the back of the truck.

Krista opened it and passed around sandwiches, soda, and chips. "There's cookies in here too, and water."

"Good, I'm hungry," said Aspen. She turned to Joey. "So, Krista thinks we should cross the bridge—the cool bridge—on the outside. What do you think?"

"I think you're crazy. I've heard of people doing that—one kid even got killed a long time ago."

Aspen turned to Krista. "I rest my case."

Krista shrugged. "I still think it would be fun to try."

The three sat in silence munching on sandwiches and chips. Finally, Aspen said, "I'm sorry this was a waste of time today."

"It wasn't a waste of time! I enjoy coming up here and it's nice to have some company that's not my brother or friends," said Joey.

"Do you have a girlfriend?" asked Krista.

"Naw, I have lots of friends that are girls, but no one like that. When I graduate I am going to join the Navy, so I don't see any sense in getting all caught up in a relationship."

"Maybe you will come to California—there's a base there." said Aspen.

Joey nodded. "Yeah that would be cool. My uncle is in the Navy, I've wanted to join since I was a little kid."

spspspspspspspspspspspsp

Aspen stopped chewing her cookie. She listened.

She heard it again. *spspspspspspspspspspspsp*

"Ummm can you guys here that?"

Joey and Krista stopped talking and turned to Aspen.

The trees rustled softly from the breeze and there was indiscernible talking coming from one of the camps nearby.

"The trees or the campers?" asked Joey.

Aspen shook her head. "Neither. It's like whispering." She closed her mouth and made the sound by quietly hissing through her teeth. "Kind of like this."

spspspspspspspspspspspsp

Joey and Krista were shaking their heads.

"You honestly can't hear it?" Aspen's voice rose an octave.

"No, Aspen, honestly. But...but maybe that's what Grandma was talking about."

"Seriously?" said Aspen. "What is it supposed to mean? Just some dumb whispering." She popped the rest of the cookie in her mouth and sighed.

Krista began cleaning up the lunch. "Hey what kid was killed, Joey?"

"Oh, it was a long time ago—he and two friends were messing around on the bridge and he fell in the river." Joey closed the tailgate and he and Krista climbed back in the truck.

Aspen hesitated next to the open truck door. She looked up through the trees toward the sky. The trees gently swayed and their leaves rustled. She shrugged and climbed into the truck and closed the door.

Joey started the engine, turned the truck around and slowly rolled along the dirt road.

Before they went around the bend putting the Quaking Aspens out of sight, Aspen turned and looked back. Nothing looked any different, but as she turned around she saw a flash of light in the side mirror, most likely the glare from the sun.

But then she heard it, *spspspspspspspspspspspsp.*

4

THE UNEXPECTED

GRANDMA WAS SITTING in the same rocker as she had been when they left, but she obviously had not been there all day because she wore a different dress and different slippers.

Krista bound onto the porch, "Did Dad and Aunt Kay make it back yet?"

Grandma shook her head. "No," she said flatly. "But they called. They found me a place in Castle Dale."

"Is that bad?" asked Krista.

Grandma's eyes clouded and her voice fell, "Anything but this home is bad," she said softly.

Krista sat down next to her great-grandma and hugged her shoulders. "I don't blame you, Grandma. I'm sorry."

"I remember seeing a sign to Castle Dale on the way to Orangeville, so is it close?" asked Aspen.

Grandma nodded, "It's close. Yes, it's close. I guess this is the price you pay for living so long, everyone has gone on ahead of you."

"Well," began Aspen. "Then they will be waiting." She tried to sound enthusiastic.

Grandma nodded, "But not at that home." Suddenly she perked up, "Aspen what did you hear in the trees?"

Aspen wrinkled her nose. "Not much. I don't think I have a sixth sense thing."

Grandma's eyes twinkled as she nodded her head. "Trust me, I am never wrong about this kind of thing."

"That's what Joey said," said Krista.

Aspen took a deep breath and blew it out as she spoke. "The only thing I heard was *spspspspspspspspspspspspsp,* and that makes no sense at all."

Grandma's entire expression changed. Her eyes narrowed looking a bit mischievous and she reached for and grasped one of each of their hands.

Krista and Aspen exchanged a quick look.

"That's it? That's all she was supposed to hear?" asked Krista.

"Did you or Joey hear it as well?" asked Grandma.

"No, not even." Said Krista.

Grandma's head slowly bobbed up and down and her bony hands released the girls. "Exactly." She said.

She looked down, folded her hands in her lap and said nothing more on the subject.

The girls were silent for a few minutes and then Krista said, "We are going to the bridge." She hurriedly added, "Dad said it was okay."

Grandma looked up. She smiled, "Okay, but be careful. It's a dangerous bridge if you don't respect it."

"Okay, we will." Aspen stood and Krista gave her grandma a quick hug.

"We'll be back in a little while, Grandma."

Grandma nodded. "Okay."

The two girls each grabbed a water bottle from the cooler and skipped down the steps.

When they were some distance from the house, Aspen said, "Maybe your Grandma is just old and isn't sure what she is talking about—you know with the whispering stuff in the trees."

"She is old," Krista chuckled. "And you're probably right. She turned to wave at her grandma and Aspen turned too.

Great Grandma was gone, her chair slowly rocking in her absence.

"Guess she decided to go inside."

Aspen nodded. "Yeah, I feel bad for her. She really doesn't want to leave her house." She sighed. "This makes me not want to live to be ninety!"

Krista linked arms with her friend. "We are both going to be ninety and we will still be surfing!"

"Best friends forever," said Aspen and she linked pinky fingers with Krista.

Krista nodded, "Yep, forever and ever." Then she added, "Hey, we can go to an old person's home together!"

They both laughed as they turned onto Main Street.

It was late afternoon now, and the sun set low in the sky west of the river from where they would be, leaving the east side of the bridge in the shade.

As they approached, Aspen marveled at the simple beauty of the structure. The narrow one-lane bridge was old, it's steel open canopy separated into two sections. A wide beam on both sides of the sections supported five narrower beams and all connected to a cross beam along the top on each side. Smaller beams across the top spanned the width of the bridge and intricate steel cables latched it all together. The two massive sections joined in the center of the bridge with wooden rails on both sides, a kind of lattice work of wood from one end to the other. The walking path on the west side was enclosed by another, only taller, wooden railing.

They carefully made their way down to the side of the bridge through the boulders as they had before. The sound of the river again, was deafening, and the spray from the crashing water was starting to get them wet.

Krista yelled, "If we move over here the water can't reach us! See!" she pointed to the dry dirt next to one of the huge cement blocks anchoring the bridge securely in place.

Aspen's heart was pounding. She nodded as they made their way to the edge of the block.

Krista pointed to the cable. "Look!" she yelled, "It's right there. We can hold on to the beams!"

Aspen stared at the side of the bridge. She wasn't sure how far beneath the bridge the water was, but she *was* positive the water was deep. Krista was right, there were plenty of places to hang onto the side of the bridge, but the cable they would be inching across on was only about as big as a garden hose. Maybe a little bigger. She could see that the spray was reaching the cable in some places.

Aspen yelled, "Krista that cable is probably slippery!"

Krista nodded, "I know so we have to hang on tight!" She started to climb up the side of the bridge. "C'mon! Its' not far to the other side!"

Aspen was shaking and she could not believe Krista wasn't scared. She put her hand on the cement pillar as Krista had done and in seconds the two were standing side-by-side on the cable. They grasped the metal beams and Krista started to slowly make her way across, side stepping inches at a time. She had cleared the dirt embankment and was now over the water.

Aspen followed. She did not dare to deliberately look down at the water, but she had to look at her feet and the pounding water was right below them.

The girls moved slowly, sliding one foot sideways, and then bringing the other to meet it, not lifting their feet from the cable. They were almost half-way.

Suddenly the bridge began shaking. They both jerked their heads up. A car was crossing the bridge causing the cable to bounce under their feet and the steele frame to shake. They both put their heads down and held on tighter, not daring to move for fear of being thrown off.

Before Aspen ducked, she noticed the driver of the car, and elderly woman, was looking straight ahead. Had she turned in the girls direction, she surely would have noticed them as they were not hidden behind the open beams.

As the car exited the bridge, the bouncing slowly stopped, and Aspen breathed a sigh of relief. She and Krista exchanged a nervous look. There was no use trying to talk, even if they yelled as loud as they could, it would be impossible to hear each other over the water.

After what seemed like several minutes, the bridge stopped moving, and they continued on their excursion.

Still cautious, Aspen's heart settled a little. *This is kind of cool.* She smiled feeling glad she had taken the chance.

Almost at the same time the bridge began shaking again and the girls froze.

Krista glanced up at the vehicle that entered the bridge. Suddenly she ducked, crouching farther down but as she did she looked at Aspen. "My dad!" she yelled.

Aspen crouched lower. She didn't hear Krista, but she read her lips. Jim Steele's truck must be the vehicle causing the bridge to shake, this time more violently than before. The first car had driven slowly across the bridge, but the truck sped across. The cable beneath the girls feet bounced violently and Aspen clung tighter to the cold beams.

They were both getting soaked from the spray as they were stopped right where the water crashed over a protruding boulder sending water in every direction.

The truck exited the bridge almost as quickly as it had entered, but the bridge did not stop shaking.

The girls both wrapped their arms around a beam closest to them.

Aspen felt like she was going to throw up. Still crouched, her legs started to hurt from the position she was in. The bridge slowly came to a rest, but the cable still moved. It was gently swaying this time, and Aspen noticed the cable was attached to the bridge in only four places. It did not bend, but there was enough give it slightly moved back and forth. The impact of the truck had a stronger affect than the slow-moving car had. The thought occurred to her the bridge designer did not expect people to use the cable as a crossing.

She took a deep breath and looked over at Krista. Her face now expressed fear and Aspen wondered if it was the bridge, or her dad, that caused that look.

They inched farther across the cable and were within a few feet from the cement pillar and dirt embankment on the other side, when suddenly a siren shrieked from farther up Main Street. The sound jolted both of them, but Krista was already stepping off the cable.

But she didn't get a chance. Instead, she flew backwards crashing into the rushing river.

"Krista!" Aspen screamed. She tried to hurry, but she was afraid she might fall too.

She glanced down just as Krista disappeared under the water.

"Krista!" she screamed again. Sobbing as she reached the end of the cable, Aspen leaned against the cement pillar and jumped onto the dry dirt next to it. She turned back to the water but could not see her friend. She fumbled in her jeans pocket for her cell phone. Her hands were shaking as she tried to unlock the screen with wet fingers.

She could barely see the phone through her tears, as she rubbed the screen against her jeans, but they were soaked too. The screen remained black.

She felt something touch her shoulder and she spun around.

"Krista!"

Aspen could not believe her eyes. She glanced back at the water and then turned back to face her friend. Krista was drenched but she was standing right in front of Aspen.

Aspen pulled her into a tight hug. "But how? What? You were in the water! You fell!"

Krista did not respond, and Aspen suspected she couldn't even hear her.

They embraced for several seconds. Aspen wasn't sure if it was her heart or Krista's pounding against her chest.

Both sobbing, they sank to the dirt. They did not try to talk, they just wept.

Aspen wasn't sure how long they sat there, but it must have been a while because the sun was setting, and the shadows of the bridge loomed over them.

They made their way up the embankment and quickly crossed the road to the walking path. There was not a car in sight.

Once they were safely on the path, Aspen asked. "How did you get out of the water?"

Krista still looked dazed. "I…I don't know. I was under the water and then I was there." She pointed to the other side. " I didn't see or hear anyone, or anything. I have no idea."

Aspen stared at her friend.

Finally, Krista said, "I know. I know." She sighed. "Well, actually I don't know."

They both started to cry again, and Aspen draped her arm across Krista's shoulders. "Let's go."

They walked along the path, and as they stepped off, they stopped and looked back.

"Well, we did it." Said Aspen.

"Yeah we did. But we are the only ones who know! We have no pictures, and we can't tell anyone! My dad will kill me—you know since I almost drowned."

Aspen laughed. "That's true, but we know! And we can tell our grandkids about it when we are ninety!"

Krista laughed too, but then tears leaked down her cheeks. "Geez, that was scary."

Aspen nodded as they started to walk again. But then she heard it and she glanced back, *spspspspspspspspspspspspsp*

When the girls got closer to Great Grandma's house, they saw evidence of the siren. An ambulance was parked on the street in front.

They arrived at the house but stayed on the front porch. It wasn't long before the paramedics exited the house carrying a stretcher, a sheet covering their precious cargo. Jim Steele and his cousin Kay followed them out the door. They didn't walk to the ambulance, instead they both sank into one of the rocking chairs.

"Dad? What happened?" asked Krista.

Dad shook his head slowly. "We were on our way home; I called Grandma a couple of hours ago to let her know we had found her a place. Then Kay called to see if we could pick her up some Mexican food for dinner…" he paused. "She likes a place in Castle Dale."

"She answered," said Aunt Kay. "But she sounded so weak. All she said was, thank you but I'm going home."

"So, we hurried home." said Jim.

Krista and Aspen exchanged a knowing look. The violent shaking of the bridge.

Krista's eyes widened. "Did she…"

Dad's head jerked up. "No, no, Krista. She had a heart attack."

Krista sighed and so did Aspen.

"She didn't want to go to the home—that… that home," said Krista.

Aspen added, "We talked to her before we went to the bridge. She was fine."

"We know," said Kay. "I guess she made the decision to not go after all."

"Can people actually choose when—to die?" asked Krista.

Dad shrugged, "I don't know. Maybe she just quit fighting."

"When we talked to her it seemed like the thing she was most concerned about was whether Aspen *heard* anything in the trees."

Dad and Aunt Kay both seemed to be waiting for Krista to go on.

"Uh, only the leaves kind of whispering. Nothing really." Aspen quickly added.

Dad and Aunt Kay both nodded but then turned their attention back to Great Grandma.

One week later, after Minnie Steele's funeral, to which the entire town of Orangeville turned out for, Krista and her dad and Aspen left for Salt Lake City and the flight home to California.

Aunt Kay stayed back to complete the sale of her Grandma's house, which they already had a buyer for, and she and her cousin, Jim Steele, agreed they would probably never have a reason to return to Orangeville. Grandma Minnie was the last relative they had there.

When Krista's dad drove the rental truck across the bridge—both girls smiles widened into grins. Maybe one day they would tell Krista's dad about their harrowing adventure when they crossed the bridge on the outside, but not today. The girls determined after Krista fell into the river, it could only have been an angel that saved her, and they weren't quite sure how to explain it to Krista's dad, especially since they could not understand it themselves.

But Aspen wondered, could the angel have been Grandma Minnie? She would suggest the thought to Krista someday, but she was not sure when that day would be. Even though Krista accepted Aspen's seemingly visions of people no one else could see, Aspen wasn't sure Krista was ready to suggest her Great Grandma might be one of them.

Jim Steele turned the truck onto the main road leading out of Orangeville leaving the bridge, and the small town, behind them.

Aspen thought back to just before the girls climbed in Joey's truck the day they drove up to the trees.

"Aspen," Grandma Minnie had said. "Listen."

OUR BUDDY JAKE

(we were fourteen)

ONE OF THEIR GOOD FRIENDS was not much of a surfer, but he was always with the beach crowd, and considered part of their 'group'. Everyone loved Jake. He was the kindest one of all. Always helping the elderly people on the beach; setting up chairs, spreading their blankets. That was Jake Davis. They all teased him saying he was bucking for one of the wealthy Elderly to adopt him and when they died leave him an inheritance. He insisted he was just a nice guy. His friends knew his motives were honorable, but they still teased him.

There was a reason Jake didn't surf. When he was five years old doctors discovered he had a condition called Cardiomegaly, which in terms we understood, was an enlarged heart, which limited Jake's participation in vigorous physical activities. On top of everything, his parents relationship seemed to be on again and off again, something Aspen had never experienced, so she did not understand what he was going through, but she and the rest of their friends tried to be empathetic. One morning, to everyone's surprise, Jake announced he was moving to San Jose. Aspen and Krista were fourteen, Jake had barely turned sixteen. But he said he would be back. They hoped and anticipated he would. Especially Aspen. She'd had a secret crush on Jake since middle school.

6

LIONS, TIGERS, AND BEARS— WELL ACTUALLY GIRAFFS

(we were fifteen)

ASPEN THREW THE CAR DOOR OPEN and Krista slid onto the back seat next to her.

Noah glanced back from the front seat. "Are you ready for this adventure?"

Krista laughed, "I can't wait! Lions and tigers and bears, oh my!"

"Wow." Aspen laughed at her enthusiastic friend. She tapped her dad on the shoulder as he steered the truck into the street. "Now why are we doing this Dad?"

"Something different than the beach. Your mom thought it would be fun."

Noah groaned.

Krista lightly tapped the back of Noah's head. "It will be fun! We're sleeping in tents, I think."

"You are." Dad chuckled. "Both moms insisted we pay for two tents—one for boys and one for girls."

Aspen sighed. "Noah is my brother."

"And practically mine!" said Krista. "But it's okay. We want our own tent anyway!"

"Well, it's because Derrick is coming," said Dad.

"Oh yeah, true." said Krista. "Where is Derrick, anyway?"

"He and his dad were in San Diego last night, so they're meeting us at the Wild Animal Park."

Aspen had not been back to this particular park since she was nine years old when she and Krista were there with Krista's aunt.

She locked eyes with Krista. It was as if their minds suddenly connected.

"The earthquake!" they said in unison.

Noah looked at Dad who laughed.

Noah shook his head. "I'm glad Derrick will be there—I might lose my mind otherwise."

"Oh, you love us!" Krista laughed heartily.

Aspen changed the subject. "What are we going to be doing exactly, Dad? Do you know?"

Jackson Allen glanced in the rearview mirror at his daughter. "It's called Roar and Snore—what does that tell you?"

Aspen raised her eyebrows; but said nothing.

When they arrived at the park, Derrick and his dad pulled in right next to them.

Noah threw the door open and jumped out as Dave Stanton opened his window. "Ready for the animals?"

"Oh yeah we're ready." Noah laughed.

Aspen walked around the back of the truck. Dave's relaxed attitude never ceased to amaze her. Nothing seemed to rattle this guy. Derrick looked like his dad but had his dad's and his mom's disposition; a little more hyper but at the same time laid back. It was an interesting combination.

Dave got out of the car and grinned at Jackson. "This was Suzann's idea?"

Jackson nodded. "Yeah she thinks the kids needed something away from the beach."

Dave grinned at his son. "Well, don't get eaten."

Derrick scoffed. "Oh, okay, Dad. We'll try not to."

Krista met Derrick as he walked toward them and linked arms with him. "We'll protect them."

Derrick clutched his heart in mock anxiety. "Oh, thank you, Krista! I feel so much better now."

Jackson shook his head. "I'm sure you do."

The four kids pulled their sleeping bags and duffle's out of the vehicles.

Jackson turned to Dave. "Are you working in San Diego this weekend?"

Dave leaned against his car. "Yeah for a few days. I'm helping them implement a new junior lifeguard program. They have a new director, and he wants to make some changes."

"They were smart to call you. San Clemente's program is one of the best."

A grin spread across Dave's face. "Yeah I kinda think so."

Jackson laughed. "It is."

"We'll meet you up there, Dad!" Noah called over his shoulder as the four kids started up the path to the check in area.

Their dads followed.

"Hey Jackson, I was wondering if I could borrow your kids next weekend. I'll check with Krista's mom too. I would like them to help me with some of the younger kids down there."

"What about the program in San Clemente?" asked Jackson. "Is it going to be okay if they miss?"

"They won't miss anything. They'll do drills in San Diego with me." Referring to his assistant Dave continued, "But that being said I wondered if you would give Jerry a hand up there for the weekend."

Jackson nodded. "Sure, I can do that."

"Thanks, man. It will really help me out."

<hr>

Aspen looked around at the group of teenagers. "There must be a hundred kids here."

"Or more," said Krista. "Do we have to share tents with them?"

Derrick and Noah joined the girls.

Noah was opening a brochure. "It says here we have four-man tents."

"So, we do share?"

"Hold on Aspen I'm still reading." He put his finger on the brochure. "No, we don't. It says two people to a four-man tent, so we have room for bags and stuff." He looked up from reading. "Ooooo—there is a midnight walk behind the scenes. Says here we go behind where the animals sleep."

Krista's eyes widened. "Is that safe?"

"Not *in* where they sleep—*behind*." Derrick emphasized for Krista.

Aspen looked at her friend. "Are you afraid?"

Krista stood erect. "I'm not afraid! I don't want to get eaten."

"Which equals afraid." Noah laughed.

Jackson and Dave joined their kids carrying lanyards, navy blue sweatshirts and aluminum water bottles with the image of an elephant and the words 'Wild Animal Park' embossed on the side.

Dave handed a bottle to Derrick along with a black marker. "Here, write your names on these. They were fifteen bucks each." He handed one to Krista.

"It wasn't included?"

"It's my present to you, Krista. You know since this may be your last hurrah…"

Everyone laughed as Krista grabbed the marker from Derrick.

"Very funny! I'll show you guys—I'll *ride* one of those elephants!"

Aspen whispered to her friend. "I actually think it's an option."

Krista's eyes narrowed. "I doubt that." But then she gave Aspen a side-glance, "Do you think?"

"We'll see." Aspen smirked.

The kids said goodbye to their dad's and proceeded to wend their way through the tents to the two they had been assigned.

"Here's ours!" Krista slapped the canvas.

"Yours will be over there."

They all turned to see who was talking.

"I'm Shirl—short for Shirley." The darkly tanned girl looked right past Krista and Aspen and reached for Derrick's hand while at the same time grinning at Noah.

Derrick's eyes lit up. It was obvious Noah was just as intrigued.

Aspen glanced at Krista who rolled her eyes.

Suddenly Krista stepped up to the girl. "I'm Krista—Shirl—eeee."

Shirl glared at Krista and opened her mouth to say something as another girl who seemed to know Shirl, approached them.

Aspen turned to greet the new arrival. "I'm Aspen, this is my brother Noah and our friends Krista and Derrick."

The new girl raised her eyebrows. Then she narrowed her eyes at Shirl.

"Brother?" she said sarcastically.

Shirl flipped her long red hair with her hand and spun on her heel. "Whatever."

She walked away with the new girl right behind her.

Noah and Derrick exchanged puzzled looks.

"What's wrong with you?" Noah asked Krista.

Krista shrugged. "Nothing." She unzipped the tent and stepped inside. "Boys are so stupid," she mumbled.

Noah and Derrick's blank looks made Aspen laugh. "Go find your tent. We'll be there in a few minutes."

The two boys shrugged and walked away.

Aspen opened the tent flap and stepped inside. "Whoa. It's hot in here."

Krista began unzipping the windows. "I don't like them."

Aspen chuckled. "Uh… that was a quick decision."

"She is a sarcastic creep."

Aspen realized Krista was really upset. "Her friend seemed…"

"She might be, but she hangs around with Shirl—" she spun around to face Aspen and blurted, "eee."

Aspen stared at her friend for a few seconds and then they both burst out laughing.

"Might be what?" asked Aspen.

"Might be nice, you were going to say nice, right?"

Aspen grinned. "No, I was going to say she might be a total weird-o."

"Oh, you were not. You think everyone is nice."

"No, I don't. Billy Campbell. I don't think he's nice."

"He isn't!"

"Exactly my point!"

Aspen sighed.

"Hey, are you guys coming?" Noah called from outside the tent. "We're starving."

Aspen lifted the tent flap. "Coming."

Derrick motioned toward Krista and gave Aspen a questioning look.

Aspen shook her head and mouthed. "It's nothing."

Krista suddenly stepped around Aspen and confronted the boys. "Don't talk about me like I'm not here."

"We weren't. You ARE here." Derrick pulled Krista into a head-lock and ruffled her hair and they all started laughing.

Derrick released her. "You are such a toughie."

Krista shrugged. "Whatever."

7

MEAN GIRLS

"CHECK OUT THIS SPREAD!" Derrick was unashamed of his exuberance regarding the tables of food before them.

"So, what? Your dad doesn't feed you?" said Krista.

Derrick picked up a paper plate as well as a hot dog and a hamburger bun, "he does, usually not this much at once."

The scratching sound of a microphone being engaged drew all of their attention to a large rock fireplace at the far end of the outside eating area. The man at the microphone looked to be in his late twenties or early thirties.

With bulging muscles and sleeve tattoos on both arms he looked like he might have been a drill sergeant and seemed as intimidating as the comparison would expect.

"Welcome to Roar and Snore!" he boomed. "My name is Chance. Hopefully, you are ready for some fun and adventure!"

He paused while the group clapped and cheered, and then continued. "To my right you will notice two large orange coolers—one is full of hot chocolate and one is orange juice. These will be available all night as will an endless supply of doughnuts. Bottled water is in the blue cooler on the ground."

"Sweet!" Derrick's loud comment made everyone laugh.

Well almost everyone. Aspen noticed Shirl and her friend across from them. Her friend was laughing but Shirl was scrutinizing Aspen and Krista.

Krista noticed too and she leaned closer to Aspen. "Oooo, mean girls."

Aspen chuckled. "Jealous mean girls."

Shirl glared at Krista.

In true Krista form, she leaned forward, glared at Shirl, and opened her eyes wide—more like bug eyes.

Aspen laughed and grabbed Krista's arm—"Lets' eat."

When they finished lunch and were clearing their plates, Noah walked up behind his sister. "Looks like you two have some new friends already!"

Aspen grinned. "Oh, I think their friendship is directed to you and Derrick. Such sweet girls." She said sarcastically.

Noah's face suddenly turned sullen and now he whispered. "She seems a little extreme to me."

Aspen turned to face him. "Seriously—they're harmless."

Noah signed. "I'm not so sure. They are a little off…"

"We will be with you the entire time."

"Not at night."

Aspen nodded. "Okay." She glanced around but Shirl and her sidekick were no-where to be found.

"Hey!" Krista and Derrick walked up to them and Krista presented two tickets.

"What are those for?"

Krista handed one to Aspen. "For a Safari. There are a lot of kids going but we have a jeep all to ourselves."

"Well with a driver," added Derrick.

"Why do we have to have tickets?" asked Noah.

"Our parents paid extra for them." Krista pointed to a young girl with a Wild Animal Park vest on. "She gave them to us."

"When do we go?" asked Noah.

"One-thirty, so we have twenty minutes. Lets' go back to our tents and maybe get things organized for night," said Krista.

Derrick and Noah showed the girls where their tent was—six or so spaces away from the girls. It was then they all noticed they were located on a huge grassy area between the lions and the elephants.

Tall fences surrounded the elephant enclosures, and the lions were fully contained behind glass.

Derrick pointed to the lions. "Do you suppose they are the roar, and they are the snore?" he continued pointing to the elephants.

"I think we're the snore," said Noah.

Derrick nodded. "Oh." He unzipped the tent but before he stepped inside he stopped. "Hey, check this out."

The other three crowded around the tent opening as Derrick picked up a box of donuts from the tent floor. He unfolded the note on top of the box and read out loud, "*your secret admirers.*"

Krista rolled her eyes. "Oh brother. Subtle are we?"

Derrick opened the box as Noah reached over his shoulder snatching a donut from the box. "Dunford chocolate, chocolate. My favorite," he said, and he took a huge bite.

"Hopefully, they're not poison," said Aspen.

"No, that will be the box they leave you," called Noah as she and Krista walked away.

Aspen and Krista approached their tent and Aspen zipped it open.

"Those two are getting on my nerves," said Krista.

"We don't actually have any proof it was..." she stopped. "Holy cow!"

Both girls stared at the mess inside their tent.

Sleeping bags unrolled and unzipped and strewn with crushed soda crackers; every piece of clothing dumped from their duffle bags and tossed about the tent.

"Ahhh!" Krista started to yell but Aspen quickly covered her friend's mouth with her hand.

"We don't want them to know it bothered us." Then Aspen whispered. "And we have no proof it was them."

Noah and Derrick walked up behind them.

"What's up?" asked Noah.

Aspen stepped away from the door so the two boys could see inside.

"This is what's up," hissed Krista.

"Whoa! What happened here?" asked Derrick.

"I wonder." Krista pushed past Derrick. "Our little note was missing though."

Aspen quickly zipped the tent shut. "C'mon we're going to be late."

Noah took hold of Krista's arm. "Hey, we don't think what happened back there is funny."

Krista sighed. "I know it, Noah. They just bug me. It's obvious those girls want to get to know you and Derrick and I guess we are in their way."

Noah let go of her arm. "I don't care if you are in their way."

Krista blushed and Aspen and Derrick, both grinning, glanced at each other.

Aspen had known for some time that Krista had a crush on her brother, and it appeared Derrick knew it, which meant Noah probably knew it too.

Wait, does he have a crush on her too? Aspen had not considered the possibility. The three of them had been best friends for what seemed like forever. Krista seemed more like a sister to them, but the reality was she *was not* their sister.

Aspen surveyed her friend and her brother who now were talking to the jeep driver whose nametag said J-e-p.

"Jed?" Krista was asking when Aspen and Derrick caught up to them.

The handsome twenty-ish African American driver chuckled. "Jep. With a p." The minute he spoke they knew he was Jamaican.

"Who would…"

Jep interrupted Krista. "Name their kid Jep?" he laughed. "My parents obviously."

"Is it…?" started Noah.

"Short for something?" he laughed again. "Nope it's just Jep. Jep Butters."

"Guess you have been asked those question before," said Derrick. He climbed onto the front seat and glanced back at Noah who was waiting for Krista and Aspen to make up their mind where they were sitting. Finally, Noah plopped in the middle of the back seat and the two girls sat on either side of him.

Derrick waited for them to get settled and then yelled, "Shotgun!"

"Yeah, we noticed," said Noah.

"We can switch later, if you want to." Derrick winked at Aspen.

Noah, who for the most part was shy when it came to girls, rolled his eyes at both of them.

Krista hadn't noticed. She was still busy being irritated at the unknown culprits who had destroyed the tent.

Jep talked to another driver for a couple of minutes, then climbed into the driver's seat. "In answer to your question, man, yes, I have been asked those questions since I can remember and no, I haven't thought of changing it."

"We didn't ask if you had," said Noah.

Jep laughed. "Nope but you were going to weren't you, man?"

The four exchanged knowing looks. That was exactly what they were going to ask him.

The two-hour Safari through the park proved to be not only fun but interesting.

The park had a railway for taking guests on tours throughout the park but what the public didn't see was another road below the railway—not visible from the track. The jeeps used that road for private tours—bringing those visitors closer to the animal enclosures.

Jep was full of information about each species of animal and had no problem answering any of their questions. When they arrived at the giraffe enclosure—Jep handed each of them a small bag of feed for the giraffes and the four climbed out of the jeep.

They turned when another jeep approached them. It was the infamous Shirl and her sidekick. The jeep stopped and the two girls jumped out.

Shirl ran up to Noah who had started up the ladder leading to a platform to feed a giraffe. She jumped onto the lower rung ahead of Krista and followed him to the top.

Noah hadn't noticed it wasn't Krista behind him. When he reached the platform and turned, he was face-to-face with Shirl.

He glanced down the ladder to where Krista and Aspen were glowering at him and he put his hands out to both sides, "What?"

Shirl wasted no time talking to him. She pulled him closer to the giraffe and held her hand out to feed it. Noah turned away from her and was down the ladder in seconds, but Krista and Aspen had already climbed another ladder.

Noah rolled his eyes as he approached Derrick and Jep who were both standing by the jeep.

"Aggressive one, she is." Jep's Jamaican accent made this statement even funnier and the three of them laughed.

Shirl's friend had been standing near the back of the jeep but now approached the two boys. "What school do you guys go to?"

"Uh, San Clemente," said Noah.

"I'm Trish," said the girl. "That's cool, actually, I thought I overheard someone say that. I…" she motioned to Shirl who was approaching them. "We just moved there."

Derrick and Noah exchanged blank looks.

"Really?" said Noah.

Shirl walked right up to them and joined in the conversation, "Yeah, her family moved there—I'm living with them."

"Shirl is my cousin," added Trish.

Derrick pursed his lips but nodded. He looked over to where Aspen and Krista were walking toward them. He abruptly walked around the front of the jeep. "You guys good with the giraffes? Let's move on. Jep was saying something about a sugar baby."

Noah climbed in the back seat. Krista walked around front of the jeep to the other side purposely avoiding the two girls, but Aspen walked right in front of Shirl, brushing her shoulder with her own.

"Oh, excuse me." Aspen's comment was dripping with sarcasm.

She stepped into the jeep and sat down.

Jep laughed heartedly. "Let's go see the sugar babies!" He looked at Derrick and laughed even more. "Sugar Gliders, man. Sugar Gliders."

"Oh. Well, I was close."

Krista slapped him on the shoulder. "Not that close."

As the jeep pulled away Aspen looked back. Shirl and Trish were standing side-by-side staring after them.

8

SABOTAGE

Krista was still talking about the little sugar gliders when they got back to their tent. Derrick and Noah had gone to grab sweatshirts before they all went to dinner.

"I so want one of those. Do you think it's possible?"

Aspen threw her a side glance. "I sincerely doubt it."

They rounded the path to their tent but stopped short. The tent flap was unzipped.

"This is getting old," said Aspen as she stepped through the door.

Krista followed her and they both surveyed the situation.

"Same mess as when we left." Sighed Krista.

Aspen started picking up her clothes. "Let's at least clear a spot for our beds. We need to shake the sleeping bags out."

Derrick and Noah arrived about ten minutes later and took on the task of shaking the crackers out of the girls beds, for which Aspen and Krista were grateful.

"Was anything missing?" asked Noah.

"It's hard to tell with this stuff everywhere. But, no, it doesn't look like it."

Derrick put Aspen's sleeping bag on her cot and smoothed it with his hands.

"What are you doing, Derrick? This is not the Ritz Carlton."

Derrick was standing next to the cot—looking around. He

answered Noah, "I know, just trying to make up for the mess. By the way, where are your pillows?"

Aspen and Krista both looked around as well.

"Those creeps." Krista snarled.

"Who?"

Aspen glared at her brother. "Oh, I don't know. Little miss prissy and her sidekick."

"Why would they do this?" said Derrick.

Aspen and Krista shook their heads.

"Seriously?" said Aspen.

Noah looked at his sister, but then quickly slugged Derrick on the shoulder. "We'll get us a place to sit."

The two boys left the tent and Krista picked up her new sweatshirt, rolled into a ball and placed it at the opening of her sleeping bag. She looked at Aspen, "boys are so stupid."

"Can you hear it?" Aspen hissed as she shook Krista to wake her up.

Krista rolled over and rubbed her eyes, "What?"

But she had no sooner said that when they saw a shadow on the side of their tent.

"It looks like a guy," whispered Aspen.

They were quiet for several seconds then Krista said, "what should we do? It's five am so it will be light soon. We don't want a lot of attention do we?"

Aspen shook her head. "No." They were both whispering but the figure outside must have heard them because suddenly it disappeared, and they heard footsteps running away.

"I am not going back to sleep." Krista sat up, pulled her knees to her chest, and wrapped her arms around them.

"Me either." Aspen sat up, spun to the side on her cot and let her feet rest on the tent floor. "Maybe I should text Noah."

"No, it's not like we are in the mountains—we are in civilization," she laughed. "Well except for the growling and roaring all night.

"I know, right? Animals are noisy!"

"And so, the term…" began Krista.

"Roar and Snore!" they both said together.

The girls decided since they were awake they may as well get dressed and go over to the eating area for some hot chocolate.

Aspen tried to unzip the tent door, but it wouldn't budge. She shined her flashlight on the zipper pull. "It's not caught in the fabric. Here," she handed her flashlight to Krista. "Can you hold this? Then I can use both hands."

Krista squatted and shined the light on the zipper. She leaned closer. "Wait a minute."

Aspen let go of the zipper and rubbed her fingers together. "It's sticky."

"I think it's honey."

Aspen lifted her fingers to her nose and smelled. "Exactly."

Krista stood and tossed the flashlight onto the cot. "Freaky Shirl—eee strikes again."

Aspen stood also. "We don't really know that."

"True, I guess maybe a bear walked over here and plastered our tent with honey."

Aspen rolled her eyes.

They both turned toward the door when they heard laughter. It was Noah and Derrick.

"Aspen?" whispered Noah.

"We're awake and no we can't get out. "

"This isn't funny but well it kinda is." said Noah.

"Can you just open the stupid door?" Krista hissed.

"Uh no reason to whisper," said Derrick. "There are a lot of people awake and they are all standing around here."

"What? Why?" demanded Aspen.

"I'll be right back." they heard Derrick say.

"Well…" continued Noah. "There are a few ropes uh—wrapped around your tent."

"What?!" shrieked Aspen but she was still whispering. She

looked at Krista who was giving her a *what are you doing look.* "I didn't want anyone to know I am freaking out."

"Why not? This is so normal. We are in a tent—with honey on the zipper, ropes tied around it and surrounded by people and intensely large animals. Why would we be freaking out!?" hissed Krista in a not so quiet whisper.

They heard giggling and laughter from outside the tent.

"This is embarrassing. I wonder how many kids are out there," said Aspen and she rolled her eyes.

"Here," Derrick said. "I'm untying the ropes you guys. It will take a few minutes."

"Yeah there are like ten ropes." added Noah.

The girls sat on their cots.

"This is *so* embarrassing." mumbled Krista.

"I don't know why we're embarrassed; we didn't do anything."

"I know; but you know what I mean."

Aspen plopped her chin in her hands. "Yeah I do."

"What's going on here?" They recognized the voice of Chance, the drill sergeant dude. He continued. "I brought these."

"Hi. Thanks." They heard Noah respond. "We don't know what's going on. This is how we found their tent."

"You girls okay?" asked Chance and they heard what sounded like shears snapping.

"Yes," said Aspen. "We're fine."

It took about five minutes for Chance to cut all of the ropes. "Is everything away from your door?" asked Chance.

The girls looked around and Aspen moved her duffle bag with her foot. "Now it is," she said.

"Why?" asked Krista.

"Well," began Chance. I'm going to try to salvage the tent so I'm putting hot water on the zipper and hopefully it will open."

"Take these and see if you can pull the zipper open." Chance was talking to someone outside the tent.

"Got it," said Noah.

Within seconds and after a few hefty tugs, the zipper opened but it fought every inch of the way. The honey was only on about a foot of the zipper so once the pull cleared the obstruction, it opened easily.

Noah handed the pliers back to Chance and leaned into the tent. "Are you guys okay?"

Krista scowled and when Noah backed away, she stepped out of the tent.

Aspen followed.

Derrick had been right. There were easily twenty kids standing around their tent, most still in pajamas or sweats.

"Unbelievable," said Aspen.

"I have a better word for it—or for them," Krista mumbled.

Noah and Derrick began the task of winding up the ropes.

Chance turned to the girls. "So, do you two have any idea who would do this?"

"Yeah…"

"Not really." Aspen grabbed Krista's arm.

Just then Shirl and Trish walked toward the group.

"Wow, what happened here?" asked Trish.

"Gee, I wonder…" Krista spat.

Shirl took hold of Trish's arm. "Bummer," she said pulling Trish with her and they walked away.

Chance looked from Aspen and Krista to Shirl and Trish but then addressed Noah and Derrick. "Can you two follow me with those ropes?"

"Sure," said Noah. He and Derrick quickly followed Chance, obviously happy for the opportunity to retreat from the scene.

Chance stopped and turned around. "Will the zipper close now?"

Aspen grasped the pull and tugged. It was a struggle at first, but she was able to close the door. She stood and looked around; everyone was gone except for two girls.

Krista glanced in the girls direction but unzipped the tent and stepped inside.

Aspen stared at the two girls waiting for them to say something.

The youngest one backed away. She looked young even for thirteen.

"I—I saw them," the girl said quietly. "They were dressed like boys—well one of them might have been a boy. It was pretty dark. I was coming back from the bathroom."

"Could you recognize them?" asked Aspen.

The girl shrugged. "I'm not sure. I'm not going to say anything until I talk to my mom." Her eyes widened, and she suddenly turned and ran behind the tents, but the older girl stayed, her gaze on Aspen.

"Well that was futile. Some help she is." Krista stepped out of the tent as the younger girl disappeared.

The older girl did not move; or say anything.

Krista grabbed Aspen's arm. "Hey, lets' go."

"Can…can you see her?"

Struggling to zip the tent again, Krista quickly surveyed the area. "Who?"

The girl turned and walked away.

"Never mind." Aspen sighed. "Yeah, let's go. We'll be leaving soon and done with Shirl and Trish."

But Krista didn't move. "Did you see someone else?"

Aspen turned to her friend and nodded. "I know, you think I'm crazy."

Krista grinned and nodded, but Aspen knew that look. Krista would not engage in conversation about what Aspen saw, she would just acknowledge, and then ignore.

Krista started to walk, and Aspen joined her as Krista said, "True. Let's go get some breakfast."

They walked side-by-side, saying nothing.

Suddenly Krista draped her arm across Aspen's shoulders and gave her a quick squeeze. The two exchanged a knowing glance as they approached the eating area.

Krista, her best friend. Nonjudgmental, always kind when Aspen had these experiences. Krista had been around for a few of them. Aspen often wondered if Krista was just being nice by not saying anything negative. Or maybe the truth was she did think Aspen was crazy and she was ignoring it. Or maybe, maybe she believed Aspen and chose to protect her. To love her anyway. To not let Aspen's peculiar sightings, get in the way of an otherwise perfect friendship. Aspen wasn't sure, but for now, she was okay with it. There may come a day when things would change but right now all was well.

As the two girls approached the eating area, they spotted Noah and Derrick who had already found them a place to sit. The girls filled their plates and joined them.

"You guys okay, Aspen?" Noah reached across the wooden picnic table and touched his sister's hand.

"Yes, we're fine. It will be good to get rid of those two girls."

Krista laughed. "I have a better description. Do you want to hear it?" Her eyes narrowed.

The other three laughed, and Derrick glanced at Noah.

Noah kicked Derrick under the table, sensing what Derrick was thinking. Trish and Shirl had moved to San Clemente.

9

RISKING DEATH TO BE SAVED OVER AND OVER

THE KIDS WERE EXCITED when they piled into Dave Stanton's truck. Derrick rode up front with his dad while Aspen, Noah and Krista climbed into the back seat.

The four teenagers were a part of Dave's Junior Lifeguard program. Because they were both sixteen, Derrick and Noah were officially on the team—but not yet (officially) a lifeguard. Krista and Aspen would turn fifteen in two and four months respectively, so they would be in the younger group of Junior Lifeguards. Still, Dave had asked the four of them to help him with a new group in San Diego so the four looked forward to a fun day in the ocean— or on the sand. Either way they anticipated fun.

Dave parked at Pacific Beach and the four jumped out of the truck leaving their boards in the back. Aspen's heart lept at the sight of at least thirty kids in red suits or swim trunks. The only difference from the suit she was wearing was the front. In place of San Clemente under Junior Lifeguard, their suits read Pacific Beach.

The Pacific Beach kids were sitting on the sand near the pier apparently listening to their instructors, one male and one female.

As they approached, both instructors turned to greet them.

The man extended his hand to Dave. "Hey Dave! Good to see you!" Dave shook his hand and introduced the four teenagers. "I brought some help along today. You know my son, Derrick."

"Hi again." Derrick grinned.

Dave continued, "This is Noah and his sister Aspen, and this is Krista." He turned to the man. "This is Ken Kiekel—Ken and I go way back."

Ken laughed. "Yeah we do, probably to these kids ages." He addressed the four teenagers as he turned back to the group of students sitting on the sand. "Thanks for coming today."

The girl standing next to Ken, in Aspen's eyes, was beautiful. Her blonde hair was knit into a tight braid that hung all the way to her waist and her blue eyes sparkled. She filled out her red one pieced lifeguard suit better than Aspen ever dared to hope she would.

"I'm Marni." The girl introduced herself.

Aspen guessed her to be in her early twenties. She glanced at Derrick and Noah who were both gawking at Marni; then she grinned at Krista and shook her head.

Krista was standing right next to Aspen and leaned into her shoulder. "Boys are so lame," she whispered.

Derrick glanced at them both. "I heard that," he mouthed.

Dave, Ken, and Marni did not seem to notice the exchange between the three of them.

After Ken quickly introduced the kids and Dave to the group, he turned the time over to Dave to outline the course of the day.

When Dave was finished he divided the students into four groups—according to their rank in the program, then he assigned Krista, Aspen, Derrick and Noah each to one of the groups. Noah and Derrick had the higher ranked groups, obviously, and Krista and Aspen the younger students.

Dave spoke into a megaphone. "We chose this beach for one reason. If we go off the point, the waves are more mellow."

"We aren't beginner surfers," blurted a kid from Noah's group.

Dave looked directly at him. "Nope you are absolutely great surfers—otherwise you would not be in this class at all, however, you are beginner lifeguards. So, you need to be in mellow waves while you train." Dave had not taken his eyes from the boy who did not respond.

"Do we understand each other?" asked Dave.

The boy looked down and nodded.

But Dave was relentless. "I said do we understand each other?"

The boy looked up. "Yes sir. I understand."

Dave nodded sharply. "Good." And then he addressed the rest of the group. "If you think this job is about looking cool, then you need to go back home, get your surfboard and go surf. There is no looking cool in saving someone's life. If you don't learn anything else from me today—*Learn that.*"

Aspen raised her eyebrows and looked over at Krista, who acknowledged with the same look.

They had never seen Dave quite so stern, and they had all worked with him for at least a year. Maybe it was because Dave had such a highly respected reputation in San Clemente and the kids never messed with him. Whatever the reason, this was a side of hippie Dave Aspen would never have thought he had.

Dave pulled a hair tie out of his swim trunks pocket and pulled his shoulder-length sun-bleached hair into a ponytail. He looped a lanyard with whistle around his neck, took three clipboards from his backpack and handed one each to Ken and Marni. He kept the third.

This was something Aspen did recognize and she knew he was ready to get down to business.

Dave picked up the megaphone and waved his hand from Noah to Derrick to Aspen and then to Krista. "These kids, are your victims." He grinned. "Don't let them die."

Derrick shook his head and looked at Noah. "I hate when he says it so casually."

Noah laughed. "It's not like we haven't done this before, and lucky me, I get the Rockstar."

Marni heard Noah and put her hand on his shoulder. "Don't worry he's harmless. He's my little brother—and that's part of his problem—I'm a little harder on him."

Derrick walked over to them. "I get it. My dad's always harder on me than the rest of the kids."

Dave walked passed them. "Not true." He smirked.

"Totally true!" Derrick called after him.

Marni walked with them to the orange cones she and Ken had set up earlier. "It is true. We are always worried about showing favoritism."

Derrick shrugged. "Yeah, well that's not a problem for my dad."

For the next two hours Aspen, Noah, Krista, and Derrick conducted physical strength and running drills with their respective groups. The drills went off smoothly with all participants scoring high. It was apparent Ken and Marni had prepared the group for this training today.

While everyone took a break loading up on bananas, protein bars and water—seven other lifeguards drove onto the sand in jeeps loaded with canoes. They headed toward the pier. Right behind them two more jeeps rolled in with three lifeguards in each who appeared to be younger than the first group.

Aspen took a deep breath and the rest of the students watched with intent.

These new arrivals were about to do their final test. Run a mile in the sand in ten minutes or less and then a one-thousand-meter swim—in this case, around the pier. They had to be at least eighteen for this and Aspen knew Noah and Derrick had to be paying close attention. This would be them in less than two years.

The lifeguards in the canoes would be out in the water when the boys did their swim to be on the lookout for any signs of problems but also as a safeguard to spot sharks that may come too close.

Aspen shivered at the thought.

It was at that second she saw the girl standing at the back of the jeep. Aspen quickly looked over at Krista, and their eyes met for a second; Aspen knew Krista understood the look on her face. She could see someone no one else could.

When the girl saw Aspen looking at her, she stared in her direction for a few seconds, then turned and walked away.

Krista caught up to Aspen and referring to their experience in

Orangeville three years earlier with Krista's great grandmother, she whispered, "Any whispering?" and she grinned.

Aspen rolled her eyes but said nothing.

For the next two hours, the four teenagers paddled out into the waves and under Dave's direction, demonstrated different types of stress situations while students in their respective groups took turns at rescue attempts. They weren't too far offshore, and even though the waves were not too rough, after ten rescues each they were all exhausted. The hardest part was not helping the rescuer—it was hard not to swim. They were also instructed to be difficult at times, to fight the rescue which they all knew people do out of fear.

When the training ended, they said their goodbyes to the students, to Marni, and Ken, and the four loaded back into Dave's truck.

"Where should we go eat?" asked Dave. "I'm buying."

It wasn't even a discussion.

"Sonny's!" they all said in unison.

The quaint popular Italian Restaurant in San Clemente wasn't as crowded as they expected on a Saturday afternoon. But it was only four o'clock and soon lines would start to form.

They claimed their table in the west front corner near the street and started pouring over the menu.

Aspen knew exactly what she wanted—manicotti. She leaned back and stretched. The west wall of Sonny's opened to the street. The only time Aspen had seen the wall closed was when the restaurant was closed. The open wall gave the feeling of being part of the activity going on outside, especially on a lazy afternoon like today. She watched the people walking by. Suddenly she froze.

Out of the corner of her eye she looked over at Krista who was still engrossed in the menu.

Aspen again looked outside. Unmistakably Shirl, and Trish, and a third girl were walking past the restaurant, but on the other side of the street. The third girl did not seem engaged in conversation with Trish and Shirl. Aspen studied her for a few seconds, she was the same girl from the beach.

Even though Aspen thought that curious, she did not dwell on the third girl; her thoughts were only about how Krista would feel if she knew Shirl and Trish had moved to San Clemente.

Aspen swallowed hard. *This can't be good. But wait, there was a street fair today. Maybe they are simply visiting.*

I hope they haven't moved here!

She turned away from the window to see Noah looking in her direction. The look on his face was all she needed.

Somehow, she knew they had.

10

Circumstances Sometimes Seem Like a Plot to Destroy Happiness—Just Because

Aspen closed the door behind her—she'd left her board by the front door while she ran back in to grab a water bottle. Krista was waiting for her on the sidewalk. The sun hadn't appeared yet even though they both knew it was there—the ocean marine layer hanging in the air would not let the sun burn off for at least three more hours.

"We're burnin' daylight!" Krista laughed. "Let's get going!"

Aspen hoisted the strap carrying her board over her shoulder and caught up with Krista. They walked down the street—around the corner and down the steep hill leading to the pier. They crossed the road and the tracks and jogged onto the sand. In seconds they were both paddling out into the cold water, lazy waves rolling past them. They weren't alone this morning—easily ten other surfers were paddling as well.

When the girls reached their destination, they turned their boards, straddled them, and faced the shore.

Aspen looked over her shoulder peering at the ocean. "The waves are kind of flat today."

Krista frowned. "They totally are, but they might pick up."

"Hopefully, this is not what the projections were for today." Aspen looked over at her best friend. Maybe this would be a good time to bring up Shirl and Trish. She had talked to Noah last night when they got home after dinner and he confirmed her worst fear. Trish's family did move to San Clemente and Shirl, her cousin, moved with her. Ugh. Aspen was not sure how to tell Krista.

Aspen was not particularly concerned about Shirl and Trish for herself, but she knew Krista would not be happy about it. It was quite obvious Shirl was interested in Noah, and even though Krista and Noah had not made anything official, after all she was only fifteen, there was no question they cared about each other. Having been friends since elementary school and at times Noah seeming more like he was a brother and not a friend—so this would be a difficult transition for them. Actually, a transition that was just starting.

Aspen took a deep breath and turned her head away from Krista, allowing the air to escape from her cheeks.

Krista was looking up at the sky when Aspen turned back around.

"Well now we have rain clouds." Krista said, "what's up with that?"

Aspen didn't respond—she knew she needed to seize this moment because once the waves started to build—the chance would be lost.

"Krista," began Aspen but then hesitated.

Krista looked at her, "What?"

"Well—I was wondering. Why do you think Shirl and Trish chose us to—I don't know, to pick on?"

"Bullying? That was sincere bullying!"

"Yeah you're right. But why us?"

"I think it was pretty clear actually—Shril likes Noah."

"You think that's the case? I mean, she moves pretty fast if it's true."

Krista rolled her eyes, "That girl is used to getting what she wants."

"Or not," said Aspen. "Maybe that's why she acts like the way she does—maybe she doesn't get what she wants all the time. So, she comes on strong from the get-go."

"Maybe." Krista sighed.

The waves were flat again. "Well at least we're getting a tan." Aspen chuckled.

"We don't need any more tan! We need surf!"

"True." Aspen glanced at her. "Okay, I need to tell you this. Since school starts next week. "

Krista eyed her friend. "What?"

"I think—well no. I know, Trish's family moved here, and I guess Shirl is her cousin and is living with Trish's family."

Krista didn't say anything which shocked Aspen. Krista was rarely at a loss for words.

What happened next also surprised Aspen.

Krista's eyes filled with tears. She glanced over her shoulder as a mild set approached them; Krista jumped to her board and caught the wave. In seconds she was yards away from Aspen.

Aspen rode the set still sitting on her board. She grabbed the next one, but like the one Krista rode, the waves weren't strong enough to take either of them all the way in.

Aspen laid on her stomach and paddled with her hands. Krista sat on her board, and Aspen easily caught her. She too pulled to a sitting position. "Are you okay?"

Krista turned to face her. "Yeah. Sorry, I just—it's just."

Aspen nodded. "Yes, all of that."

They both laughed. It was so wonderful to have a friend who understood what you didn't say.

The two were silent for a few minutes.

Finally, Aspen said, "Noah loves you Krista."

Krista sighed. "I know, but like a sister - friend, or what?"

"I guess I am saying you have a huge edge."

Krista scoffed. "Ugh—but I don't have flaming red hair! And she is pretty."

"So are you."

Krista snickered. "I guess." She plopped stomach first on her board. "Let's get in—it's starting to rain."

"When did a little rain bother you?"

"Today."

For the next week Aspen helped Krista look for Trish and Shril. When they weren't surfing they were searching. They hit the local stores, but with no success. They walked up and down El Camino Real enough times they were both quite sure they had walked a full marathon. They also trapesed up and down Avenida Pico and Avenida Del Mar too, but still no sightings of a red head with her brunette sidekick. No beach sightings either. Aspen decided maybe Shirl and Trish had not moved to San Clemente at all.

However, the Sunday before school started, Aspen and Noah drove to the local Albertsons to pick up a prescription for their mom. Aspen ran in while Noah waited in the car. He wanted to sit in his Iroc with the top down. This car was his dream and he'd only had it a couple of weeks, an early birthday surprise from their parents.

Coming out of the store she nearly ran into Trish and another girl, but not Shirl, Aspen stopped.

"So, you did move here?"

Trish frowned. "Hi to you too."

Aspen swallowed hard. "Sorry. Let's try again. Hi Trish."

Trish smiled a little. "Hi, Aspen and yes we moved here a few months ago."

"Hmmm—from where? I mean what school?"

"We moved from Temecula—I went to Temecula Valley." Trish hesitated. "Shirl moved in with us for a while because her parents are getting a divorce. She's from the valley."

Aspen smiled. "Okay then, I'll see you in school."

"Yeah tomorrow—where did summer go?"

Aspen shrugged. "Yeah. Sophomores right?"

"I am." Trish kind of winced. "Shirl is a junior. I'm not sure how long she is going to be here."

"Well—San Clemente is a great school. Do you play any sports?"

"I do, lacrosse. I don't think Shirl does though."

"Well maybe she will change her mind." Aspen stepped to the side and started for the door again but almost bumped into the girl behind Trish. She was the same girl Aspen had seen with Trish and Shirl down by Sonny's—and at the beach. Aspen stopped suddenly. "Oh, excuse me."

Trish looked startled and she glanced behind her. "Excuse you why?"

Aspen quickly looked around. The girl was gone..

Aspen stammered, "Oh, I…I almost bumped into your friend." She regretted the words the minute they tumbled from her mouth.

Trish's eyebrows furrowed. "Uh, I'm not here with anyone."

Aspen's eyes widened. "Oh, my bad. Well anyway see you tomorrow." Aspen walked quickly through the open automatic doors of the store and hurried to the car. She didn't tell Noah about the girl . She was careful about how much she told Noah, Mom or Dad about people she 'could see.'

Noah started the car. "You okay?"

Aspen looked toward the store. "Yeah, I'm good. That was Trish."

"I thought I saw her go in the store." He pulled the car onto the street. "So, she did move here?"

"Yep, and so did her cousin, mean girl Shirl."

"Eeee." Noah mimicked Shirl from that first day they met.

Aspen looked at her brother and they both laughed.

"Oh wow." Aspen shook her head. "They seriously moved here. This can't be good."

Noah glanced at her sideways but said nothing and drove out of the parking lot.

Aspen dismissed the thoughts of the elusive girl.

11

WE HAVE THE REST OF OUR LIVES

SAN CLEMENTE HIGH was not far from where Aspen and Noah, Derrick, and Krista lived. But they did have to cross the 5 freeway—rather go under it. None of their parents liked the idea so they typically drove them to school. That's how it had always been—all of their schools since elementary were east of the 5, not by the beach.

However, now Noah had his car, and was getting a small amount of money from his Junior Lifeguard training, he could buy his own gas. He and Aspen picked the other two up and they rode together. They all pitched in for gas, but Noah would have probably taken them for free—he was so thrilled to be driving his own car, and a convertible!

San Clemente was a four-year school, so this was Aspen and Krista's second year and Noah and Derrick's third.

As usual, Krista and Aspen were in all of the same classes—it had practically taken an act of congress this year, but they managed. As it turned out, Trish ended up in their third period English class. She didn't seem so bad. She took a seat near Aspen but avoided talking to Krista. Of course, Krista made it easy. She didn't give Trish so much as a nod.

The ride home from school was a little tense, but the four were in a hurry to get to the beach so the conversation lasted less than ten minutes.

In those ten minutes they all shared information about the new girls. Shirl was in three of Noah's classes and one of Derricks. Needless to say, the news didn't set well with Krista, but she didn't have much to say about it. When Noah dropped her off she jumped out of the car, waved, and announced she would meet them at the beach—her dad would take her.

After dropping off Derrick, Noah parked the car on the street in front of their house and followed Aspen inside. "What's up with Krista?"

Aspen stopped and turned around to face him. "Are you serious?"

"Yes, why is she so stand offish? I haven't done anything to her and neither has Derrick."

"She's jealous, Noah."

"Of what?"

"Of Shirl of course."

"I don't like Shirl—I mean she's cute and all, but I don't like her. She's kind of snobbish."

Aspen sighed. "Well stick with snobbish and don't mention cute and all, around Krista, okay? She is a little sensitive about this."

Noah's eyes widened. "Does Krista…"

"Like you? Seriously? Have you been on another planet?" Aspen walked into the kitchen and opened the fridge. "Want a yogurt?"

Noah nodded and she tossed him one. He pulled the lid back looking thoughtfully at his sister. "I know she cares about me, and I do her too, but I guess I had never thought about it, *that* way."

Aspen scowled. "Not even a little?"

Noah sighed. "Okay to be honest, yes. But geez we used to play in wading pools together and have sleep overs when we were little. I guess I have kind of side-stepped those feelings because we are such close friends. I didn't want to ruin that. And besides, I haven't really dated yet."

"There you have it. Shirl is sixteen and so are you—that's probably why Krista is feeling the way she is."

"Aren't you two going surfing?" Dad emerged from his office.

"Yeah—on our way." Noah turned and jogged up the stairs.

"Did I happen into a private conversation?" asked Dad.

"Not sure how private; uncomfortable maybe." Aspen kissed her dad on the cheek. "See you in a couple of hours."

"Who is on dinner duty tonight?"

Aspen moaned. "Ugh, I am. Jo will be here, right?"

"Jo is always here." Dad laughed. "Maybe I should give her the night off."

"No!" wailed Aspen, even though she knew her dad was kidding.

Jo was their maid and had been for as long as Aspen could remember. She was practically a member of the family, like a second grandma. Aspen and Noah only knew their Grandma Hansen, their mom's mother. Their dad's mom died years ago, and Dad never talked about her.

When Noah and Aspen crossed the tracks Krista and Derrick were already there. They were sitting on the sand, their surfboards standing next to them.

Krista's mood had completely changed. "Hey! We were thinking about going in without you two." She grinned and jumped to her feet. "Let's go—surf's up!"

Relief washed over Noah's face at Krista's mood swing and he grinned at his sister. "Whew."

The four trotted waste deep into the water then jumped on their boards and paddled out.

Aspen caught up to Krista. "So?"

"I'm good. I was being stupid. Noah and I will always be friends. Of course, he is going to date. I'm not going to worry about it. We have the rest of our lives."

Aspen smiled at her best friend. "That's true. We have all the time in the world."

The waves were awesome and the next two hours were filled with 'sick' surfing. Many of their friends were there too, the regulars.

They were like an unspoken organized club. They all watched each other's backs, so it wasn't surprising what happened when Shirl pranced up to them as they were all emerging from the water after their last ride.

Aspen glanced toward the pier and saw Trish walking slowly in their direction. But Shirl walked right over to Noah and grabbed his towel when he leaned over to pick it up. In doing so , she flipped sand into the eyes of those standing close by.

"What is your problem?" snapped Kimber Elliott. "No beach etiquette or what?" She grabbed a water bottle and flushed the sand from her eyes.

Shirl turned on her. "What? Afraid of a little sand?"

Brian Hollingsworth stepped between the two girls, still blinking sand from his own eyes. "Hey, that was not cool."

Shirl glared at all of them. "What a bunch of babies. You all think you are so special!"

Aspen was stunned. She opened her mouth to say something but caught Krista's 'don't you dare' look from the corner of her eye and clamped her mouth shut.

Most of their friends blew Shirl off with a shake of their heads, but Kimber was kind of a hot head and she was not standing for it. Everyone knew you never pick up a towel quickly from the sand— you lift it slowly and shake the sand off close to the ground, so it doesn't fly in everyone's faces.

Before either girl could throw any more rude comments at each other—Trish walked up behind her cousin and took her arm. "C'mon Shirl. You wore out your welcome." She glanced at the group. "She just moved here. Sorry."

Shirl didn't seem to know what to say but she didn't immediately leave.

Krista surprised Aspen when she said, "It's kind of a rule—if you pick up a towel like that it flips the sand all over. Maybe—maybe you could remember next time you come down here."

"If there is a next time," snapped Kimber.

"We don't own the beach, Kimber," Brian spoke softly to his friend.

But Kimber glared at Shirl, turned on her heel and stomped away. As she passed Aspen and Krista she looked right at Krista. "Besides, she shouldn't be messing with your guy," she whispered and kept walking.

Krista's eyes widened. "What did she say?" she hissed to Aspen.

"Hmmmm—guess it's kind of obvious." Aspen chuckled.

"Ugh." Krista rolled her eyes but stopped when she caught Noah looking directly at her.

He smiled.

She grimaced.

Then they both picked up their surfboards and walked across the sand with Aspen and Derrick.

Aspen chuckled. *And the saga continues...*

12

JAKE'S BACK

WHEN JAKE WALKED OUT of the principal's office the third week of school, Aspen was shocked but happy, like everyone else. Jake explained his parent's had tried to make things work, but his mom wanted to stay in San Jose, and his dad's entire life and family were in San Clemente and he elected to come back home.

All of their friends knew Jakes's parents had been having trouble, but they did not realize how bad it really was. Jake wanted to graduate with his friends, so he came back with his dad, his younger sister and brother stayed with their mom.

Jake seemed okay, and all of their friends rallied around him. Jake was a good guy and none of them wanted to see him sad. They drug him to the beach like always—Derrick even tried to coax him into surfing, but Jake wanted nothing to do with it.

"I'm afraid of the water." He confessed. "I'm thinking of taking up bowling."

Everyone nearby turned to him in disbelief.

"Bowling?" Noah said flatly.

"Yeah, you can't drown when you bowl."

Derrick slapped Jake on the back. "You can't drown in sand either!"

Jake had to agree, "You have a point."

The boys scooped up their boards and headed for the water, and Krista followed. She glanced back, "Are you coming, Aspen?"

"In a sec." she spread her towel next to Jake and sat on it.

"You don't have to hang here, Aspen."

"I want to! I just want to talk right now." The crush she had on Jake when they were younger had long dissipated but her warm feeling for her friend had not. She leaned into his shoulder. "I'm sorry about your parents, Jake. That has to suck."

He nodded. "Yeah, but honestly, it's better not having them fight all the time." Referring to his younger siblings he added, "I feel so bad for Jason and Julie when they fight. I only have a year of this left, then I'm going to college, but they are still in middle school."

Aspen nodded. They sat in silence and she drew little circles in the sand with her finger.

"You should go surf. I'm good, I promise. I need to find me an old lady to help."

He made Aspen laugh right out loud. She stood and picked up her board from the sand. When she turned around, she saw Shirl walking towards them.

Without so much as acknowledging Aspen, Shirl plopped down next to Jake. "I hear you like bowling," she cooed. "*I* like bowling."

Jake quickly looked up at Aspen.

She took a deep breath and then said, "Jake this is Shirl. She and her cousin just moved here from Temecula."

Shirl corrected Aspen, "I'm actually from the Valley."

"Whatever," said Aspen. "You live with Trish and she is from Temecula. Anyway, this is Jake Davis." She stopped and looked directly at Shirl, "what is your last name anyway?"

Shirl waved Aspen away with her hand. "It doesn't matter."

Aspen rolled her eyes. She did not like what was happening; like Noah and Derrick, Jake was mesmerized by the attention he was getting from beautiful Shirl. He glanced up at Aspen and grinned, raising his eyebrows as he did.

Aspen gave him a weak smile, spun on her heel rolling her eyes as she did and jogged into the water. She plopped on her board on her stomach, paddling quickly toward the other surfers.

Aspen couldn't decide which was worse—to have Krista constantly complaining about Shirl and the attention she was giving Noah, or to painfully stand by and watch Shirl lead Jake along.

For weeks Shirl sought Jake out in the halls at school, made sure she arrived at the beach right after Jake got there, and in the meantime wasted no time flattering Noah, Derrick, or any other boys who happened to be nearby. But they blew her off, chalking up her attention to her own need for approval.

But not Jake, it was obvious Jake was head over heels for Shirl, visibly causing him anxiety every time Shril turned her attention on one of the other boys. That infuriated Aspen. She was not jealous, but she loved Jake and valued his friendship—and most of all she did not want to see him get hurt. Worst of all, Shirl was always pushing him to surf, to which Jake adamantly refused. But, he had made it clear no one was to tell Shirl about his heart condition. He wanted to be treated "normal" as he put it.

One day while in English class, Krista asked Trish why she never came to the beach anymore.

"I don't surf, and I don't feel comfortable when Shirl is around you guys. I keep hoping she will move back home soon." Trish suddenly looked embarrassed, "I know I'm not being a nice person—she is going through a lot I guess, but she is so not me." She stopped talking for a second but then added, "Besides, I'm playing lacrosse and it takes a lot of my time."

"That's cool," said Aspen. "I'm glad you got back into it."

Trish grinned, "Me too, it was hard moving in high school. I wouldn't wish it on anybody. I thought having Shirl here would make it easier, but it didn't. We are not cut out of the same cloth." She hesitated, "and that Jake guy—she's using him. Just so you know."

Aspen bristled. "Why—doesn't she like him? She could probably make some friends if she wouldn't be so difficult all the time," said Aspen.

Trish shrugged, "She likes him, but she likes other boys too, he is the one showing her the most attention, but trust me, it won't last. She insists on being a brat. My mom finally told me to do what I wanted to do and not to worry about Shirl. She's a grade ahead of me in school anyway."

The bell rang and Aspen picked up her backpack. "Good luck with lacrosse, Trish, and don't be such a stranger at the beach."

Trish nodded, picked up a paper from her desk and walked up to their teacher.

Krista walked into the classroom as Aspen was walking out.

"Where did you go?" asked Aspen.

"I got a text from my mom while you were talking to Trish," said Krista.

Aspen looked at her, "and?"

"Oh! I left my activity card home and I need it to get my new sociology book, so she left it in the office for me." She changed the subject, "What did Trish say?"

"She's playing lacrosse, so she hasn't got time for the beach." Aspen flung her backpack over her shoulder, "and according to Trish, Shirl is using Jake."

"We kind of figured that."

"Yep, but I don't like having it confirmed."

It was lunchtime and the two girls exited the school and headed towards the tables at the far end of the campus, their favorite place to eat and where most of their friends met up. They saw Shirl and Jake walking in front of them.

"Hey Jake!" called Krista.

He turned and grinned. "Hey what are you two up to?"

"Uh the usual," said Aspen. "Lunch."

Jake glanced at Shril who immediately linked her arm through his.

Jake said, "Why don't we go with them? It's where I usually eat."

Aspen took a deep breath then lied, "Yeah, Shirl, you are welcome to come."

Shirl leaned into Jake and put her head on his shoulder. "Well, Jake and I were going to—you know, have a private lunch."

Krista scanned the school grounds and the hundred or so students milling about. "Yeah, good luck with that."

"C'mon, Jake." Aspen walked quickly to Jake's side and linked her arm with Jake's free one.

He surprised Aspen when he pulled away from her. "No, I mean well—Shirl and I are going to walk over to the store."

Aspen shrugged as she released Jake's arm.

Krista glared at both Jake and Shirl, "suit yourself." she snapped. "C'mon Aspen."

Krista and Aspen walked away but Aspen glanced back at Jake—at the same time Jake looked over his shoulder at her, but what had happened hurt Aspen's feelings and Krista noticed.

"Aspen, he has a girlfriend—it's okay if he has a girlfriend."

"I know—but she is not a girlfriend—she is a…a user!"

Krista nodded, "I know, but-hmm—now who is all mad about Shirl?"

Aspen sighed but then she started to laugh. "I guess you're right. I don't trust her, especially after talking to Trish."

Aspen looked back again, Jake and Shirl had disappeared from view.

By Friday, Jake had hardly spent any time with them. Their entire group noticed and had tried to reach out to Jake, but he was totally committed to spending time with Shirl and seemed uncomfortable talking to any of them about her.

Saturday morning when Aspen, Krista, Noah, and Derrick arrived at the pier they noticed Jake sitting on the sand where they usually met. He had a surfboard with him.

When they reached Jake, he looked up at them and grinned.

"Hey, Jake! Good to see you, man." Noah plopped his surfboard next to Jake's and sat down.

"Are you taking up surfing today?" asked Derrick.

Jake nodded, "yeah I think I'll try it. I have the best teachers right here, and Shirl thinks it would be cool if I could surf like the rest of you guys."

Aspen scowled. "Does Shirl know about your heart, Jake?"

Jake shrugged, "yes, I did tell her. But I'm not sure she believes me…"

"Or understands the danger!" Krista sat next to Jake and draped her arm across his shoulders. "Jake, this is stupid, really. Who cares what Shirl thinks?"

"It's true, Jake," said Noah. "She doesn't surf so why should it matter if you do?"

"It matters to me," said Jake and he turned to Krista, "I care what she thinks. I—guess she—she wants me to be like, you know, you guys."

Krista took her arm from Jake's shoulders and stared at the water. Suddenly she stood, "well this is the dumbest thing in history. We are not going to let you do this."

Aspen twisted her mouth. "Jake, we don't want you to die. Shirl just doesn't get it."

Jake suddenly jumped to his feet. "No, you guys don't get it. Shirl is the first girlfriend I have ever had, and I want her to think I'm cool."

The four teenagers didn't say anything—they didn't know what to say. Jake was a good friend, and they did not want him to risk his life for a girl he hardly knew, but it was true. In all the years they had known him, Jake had not had a girlfriend.

Jake picked up his surfboard, "so who's going to teach me?"

None of them moved—no one wanted to take Jake out into the ocean. Finally, Aspen said, "Jake, look at the swells. The waves are pretty rough today. How about we do this another day?"

Jake glared at her, but then he looked past her, and his expression changed from anger to obvious sadness. Instinctively, they all turned to see what Jake was looking at.

Shirl, with her arms wrapped around the neck of a boy they had never seen before. After a passionate kiss, with an arm around each other's waists, they walked toward the group.

Jake held onto his board, gaping at the couple.

Shirl and the new boy walked directly up to them and Shirl said,

"Hi everyone!" She didn't wait for anyone to respond. "Jake, this is Jeromy, remember, I told you about him."

Jake's mouth still gaped open; he said nothing.

Aspen looked from Jake to Shirl and back to Jake. She barely heard Jeromy say, "Hi. Shirl has told me so much about all of you."

What happened next took Aspen, Derrick, and Noah by complete surprise.

Krista suddenly bolted past Aspen and charged directly for Shirl. She slammed into her chest with both hands taking Shirl completely by surprise and knocking her to the ground.

Jeromy was thrown off balance too and stumbled to keep his footing.

Dazed, Shirl lay on her back.

Jeromy extended his hand to help her up, but Krista pushed his hand aside and stood above Shirl, glaring down at her.

A crowd was starting to gather, and Noah stepped close to Krista and took her by the elbow, but Krista shrugged him off.

"Look!" she yelled at Shirl. "I don't know who you think you are, first you kiss up to Noah and Derrick at the park when you didn't even know them, and if that wasn't bad enough, you pretend to…" she stopped and turned to Jake, "I'm sorry, Jake," she turned back to Shirl, "you pretend to like Jake and try to get him to surf, having no concern about his heart—and I don't mean breaking his heart, I mean his physical heart! You lie, you are sneaky and dishonest! YOU do not belong here!"

Shirl had not moved. She was still on her back on the sand, propped up on her elbows. She glared back at Krista but did not respond.

Krista turned to Jeromy, "we don't know you and maybe you're a nice guy, but if you are, you should run while you can. Your girlfriend is a deceiving, lying little sneak."

Jeromy glanced around at the crowd of teenagers, then he shook his head. He shot Shirl a disgusted look, turned and walked away.

"Jeromy!" Shirl screamed. "Where are you going?"

"Home!" he yelled back without turning around.

Shirl scrambled to her feet, but Krista moved closer to her, her voice lower now, calmer, "we are so done with you."

Shirl nervously glanced around the group, her eyes resting on Noah, then Derrick, and then Aspen. She tried to brush the sand from her legs and back and then she looked directly at Jake. "What do you have to say, are you going to defend me, or be the wimp I thought you were from the beginning."

Jake surprised them all when he shrugged and said, "do I know you? I don't think we've met."

The entire group burst out laughing. Everyone but Krista, she still glared at Shirl.

Shirl's face turned a bright shade of red. She glared back at Krista, then without saying another word, she turned and walked quickly away.

Jake held his new surfboard away from him, "wonder if they give refunds?"

Everyone started to laugh, some patted Jake on the back, and others high-fived him. Jake struggled to keep a positive look on his face, but as soon most of the crowd had dispersed, he sank onto the sand.

Noah knelt next to him. "Dude she is not worth it. She is not an honest person."

Jake nodded quickly, "Yeah, I know that."

Aspen knelt on the other side of him and Jake turned to her, "then why do I feel like crap?"

Derrick and Noah picked up their boards and walked toward the water. Krista hesitated. She heaved her board above her head, "Jake, I'm sorry. It's that we…we love you."

Jake chuckled, "I know—hey, you can be quite a bruiser!"

Krista blushed. "I…" she turned and jogged across the sand.

Aspen and Jake sat in silence for several minutes.

Finally, Jake said, "I feel like an idiot. You guys were probably laughing at me."

Aspen's head jerked up and she turned to face him, "Laughing at you? Are you crazy? We have all been there Jake, crushes can be so painful."

"Like you've ever had to worry about that. Anyone of you—the cool kids of San Clemente."

Aspen sighed, trying not to be offended by his comment. "Is that what you think—we think?"

Jake scoffed, "No, not what you think, it's what I think. I have always wanted to be part of you guys."

Aspen scooted closer to Jake and put her arm around is shoulders. Jake was a big guy and she had to scoot even closer to keep her arm there.

"You are one of us, Jake, you always have been. We love you and we don't care that you don't surf. Geez, it isn't everything." She stopped and said nothing for a few seconds. "But I guess we act like it is don't we?"

Jake shrugged, "I guess."

Aspen grinned. "Well, maybe we should all go bowling one night. It would be fun, too!"

Jake laughed out loud, his normal jolly laugh everyone loved. "Okay Miss Aspen, but I'll wipe you out—I'm pretty good."

"Oh, so you've been holding out on us?"

"I took my brother and sister bowling a lot in San Jose, just to get out of the house. Found out it's something I can do—and yeah I'm pretty good."

"Then it's a date."

Jake held up his fist to bump Aspen's, but she instead leaned in and kissed is cheek. "I love you, Jake."

"I love you to, Aspen, and thanks—for being there."

"Ha, don't thank me, It's Krista who thinks she's The Rock."

They both laughed and Jake said, "Take your board and get out of here, I need to find some old people to bug."

13

MAN IN THE WATER

It was almost three o'clock when Aspen and Krista pulled their boards from the water, found their towels, and plopped onto the sand.

"What an amazing day! Could the waves get any better than this?"

Krista downed a half bottle of water before answering her friend. "I don't think so, I love days like this."

The two of them along with Derrick and Noah had arrived at the pier early for Junior Lifeguard training. Once released to surf on their own, they had hit the water and except for a couple of quick breaks had been surfing all day. The sets had been steady most of the day, with a few lulls giving them all time to float on their boards and enjoy the beauty around them.

The beach was crowded and so was the water. But the locals understood protocol, so transitions from one set to another had been easy. There seemed to be very few beginners in the water today, which made it even easier on the regulars as danger of the novice surfers dropping into waves in front of the more experienced was eliminated—a predicament common to most surfing communities.

Aspen was stretched out on her towel but suddenly she sat up. She stared at the ocean for a few minutes and then said, "hey let's get another set in—looks like the tide is starting to change."

Krista immediately stood and the two hauled their boards into the water as Derrick and Noah rode into shore.

Noah called to his sister, "you guys going back out? The waves are getting a little tricky."

"Just one more set!" called Aspen. "C'mon, come with us."

"You guys hurry up—we're burnin daylight!" Krista yelled.

Noah did not have to be convinced and he and Derrick turned their boards and paddled back out with the two girls.

The four battled the rising swells to get far enough out the catch the best sets. Noah was right, the sea was getting aggressive making surfing a little more challenging—even for the most experienced surfers.

But that did not deter the four teenagers—or several other die-hards who remained in the water.

They all saw the rising swell at the same time and each of them turned their boards to be ready to drop into the next wave.

When the wave hit they all jumped to their boards; Noah, Derrick and Krista caught it easily, but Aspen's ankle strap pulled apart and she lost her board and plummeted deep into the wave. She surfaced, caught her breath, and again was pulled under water. When she surfaced this time, she caught sight of her board bouncing on the water close by. She began swimming as hard as she could to catch it, but every time she was within reach, her board bounced away from her.

She kept trying, but she was getting tired and the waves were getting increasingly rough, so she turned toward shore and began swimming. After a few yards, she flipped onto her back to rest, the turbulent water constantly submerging her face.

When she turned toward shore again, she realized what was happening. She was caught in a riptide—she saw the lifeguards had now posted the familiar red flag—warning surfers and swimmers of rough water. Only this was worse than rough water, a riptide is a strong offshore current caused by the tide pulling water through an inlet along a barrier breach, at a lagoon or inland marina where tide water flows steadily out to sea during ebb tide. The description tumbled over in her mind. They had to memorize it for the life-guard program. That was the technical term—reality for her was simply that she could not swim toward shore. Riptides were not only exhausting to a swimmer they could be deadly.

She groaned. She was definitely caught in it and she was getting farther away from shore, not closer.

Aspen knew exactly what to do—swim across the current—not against it. But she was exhausted, and it was getting harder to stay above water. She could see several people standing along the edge of the water, and she thought she saw two lifeguards coming her way. Good, they would have life preservers.

A typical ocean current would push her toward shore, but in this case, she was being pulled farther out to sea even as she swam with as much power as she had left, across the current, as she had done before in this type of situation.

Aspen closed her eyes and turned on her back. She had to rest. It was easier now, she was out beyond the dangerous current, but she could not float out here forever.

"I got you."

Aspen jerked her eyes open. The lifeguards had made it. The sun behind the man towering over her made it difficult to see his face. But she didn't recognize his voice either; she knew most of the lifeguards personally.

But wait, this guy was *standing*? What?

The man lifted Aspen from the water and laid her face down on her board. *Where had that come from?* Then he wrapped the ankle strap around his hand and began pulling her toward shore.

What was happening? She tried to focus on the man—who was he and how was he walking through the ocean? Why wasn't he swimming? She tried to watch him, but the waves caused to board to beat against her chin, so she gripped her board with both hands and laid her cheek against it, silence.

"Aspen!"

She jerked her eyes open to the sound of Noah's voice.

"Aspen, are you okay?"

She focused on her brother who was leaning over her.

Dave Stanton, Derrick's dad and over the Junior Lifeguards at San Clemente pier, slapped a cuff around her arm.

"What was that all about?" he was saying and then she heard him mumbling about the four of them going out into the water when they knew they should probably have called it a day.

"She's okay," he said to whoever was listening and leaned closer to Aspen shining a light in each of her eyes, lifting her eyelids as he did. He sat back on his heels as he removed the cuff from her arm. "Okay, kid." He patted her arm and then stood. "Can you grab her some water, Derrick?"

"Sure." Derrick turned and jogged away from them.

Aspen tried to look past all of them to find the man who had brought her in.

"Where is that guy?" she asked while Noah helped her sit up.

"What guy?"

She looked at Noah quizzically, "The guy who brought me in. I've never seen him before."

Dave Stanton started to walk away but glanced back at Aspen. "You were nearly to shore when the lifeguards reached you Aspen. There was no one else."

Krista shrugged, "It's true, there was no guy Aspen, you floated in on your board."

"Yeah how did you do that anyway?" asked one of the lifeguards. "Like Dave said, we were on our way out to get you and before we got past the swells, you floated towards us." Luke, one of the lifeguards, punched the air with his thumb towards another lifeguard, "Mason pulled you in the rest of the way."

Aspen rubbed her forehead with both hands. "Are you sure cause there was this guy?"

Noah plopped down next to his sister and grinned, "well you are delusional—it's the only explanation. There was no guy, Aspen, honest. Just Luke and Mason."

Aspen looked up at Mason and then Luke.

"Yeah, he was way bigger than you guys."

Mason laughed, "Gee thanks."

"I mean…"

Mason knelt next to her. "I'm kidding. Are you feeling okay?"

"Fine, I'm just tired."

"You were out there a long time, Aspen, you scared the crap out of us," said Krista. "I didn't even realize you weren't with us until I was all the way in."

"Sorry. My strap came off my ankle and I lost my board."

Derrick held up the strap. "It actually broke, weird."

Aspen's eyes widened. "Wow."

Luke sighed, "It happens. I'm glad this ended well."

Aspen nodded. "Yeah, me too." She looked into all of their faces. "You didn't see a man—for sure?"

They were shaking their heads, "no man, Aspen. We're sure." Said Krista, but she threw Aspen a knowing glance.

Aspen took a deep breath and slowly let it out. She started to stand, and Noah grabbed her arm and helped her to her feet.

"I'm okay, Noah, promise." She stood still for a few minutes gazing out at the water. The warning flag was still up—she could see the dangerous current, but she could not see any man.

Who was that guy?

She felt someone looking at her and she slowly turned in the direction she thought it came from. There he was, well over six feet tall, balding, and muscular. He seemed to be older than her dad.

He lifted his hand, opened, and then closed it quickly acknowledging she had seen him, then he grinned and simply walked into thin air. Vanished.

14

THE STUPID LETTER

"WHAT IS WRONG WITH DAD?" Noah walked directly up to their mother and Aspen was right on his heels. Dad had been away all day and when he came home he locked himself in his office without even acknowledging his kids or his wife.

But mom had been crying and she did not immediately answer.

"Mom?" Aspen leaned closer to their mother. "Are...are you and Dad okay?"

Suzann Allen quickly brushed tears from her cheeks. "Oh yes! It's nothing like that. It must be business."

"But, Mom, Dad has never acted like this," said Noah.

Mom nodded, "I...I know."

It was late March, and the last quarter of school was well under way. Aspen and Noah were looking forward to warmer weather and surfing without wet suits. Their parents had taken them and Grandma Hansen to Hawaii over Christmas Break. Valentine's Day came and went, and Spring Break was approaching. Dad and Mom had discussed going up the coast to Oxnard to do some sailing, but Mom wanted to stay home this year, so plans were changed. A decision Aspen did not know then but was one she would be forever grateful for.

Spring Break was the last week of April this year and Aspen and Krista had a week of surfing and shopping all planned. Derrick and

Noah were happy to participate in the surfing, but shopping did not excite either of them.

It's funny when things aren't right at home, nothing else sounds fun. Aspen and Noah were concerned about their parents. Noah brought up Jake's parents' divorce and was worried maybe something had happened with their own parents.

Mom assured them it was not the case, but even so, she did not seem to have any answers. Dad had changed. He was like a complete stranger and the upset it caused in their otherwise happy family was real, and it hurt all of them. Aspen and Noah were not sure they believed their mother. She had never lied to them before, but how could she not know what was going on with their dad? It didn't make sense.

When Dad emerged from the office at dinner time, he made an announcement that would leave his children and wife reeling.

"We're moving to Tennessee." He said flatly. "We have to leave May first."

Uncharacteristic for Mom, she slammed both fists on the center island she was standing next to and demanded to know why.

Dad's eyes narrowed. "Suzann, I'm only going to say this once. My sister, Dana, has to move. There is a…a family mansion there and it needs to be sold."

"A what? Where? Why have I never heard of this before?" The hurt in moms eyes was evident.

"It was never relevant to our life. I didn't think it ever would be." Dad's tone was softer now.

"Well, I'm not going!" Noah started to walk away but Dad grabbed him by the arm.

"You are going," said Dad. There was no compromising in his tone.

"Dad, I'll be a senior! I don't want to go to…where?"

"I know you don't want to go, Noah." Dad looked at Aspen and then at Mom. "I know none of you do. But the case is closed. We leave May first. I'm not sure for how long." His sentences were short. Abrupt. To the point.

Noah pulled away from his dad and bolted from the room. This time Dad did not try to stop him.

They heard the front door slam.

"Dad, this is stupid." Aspen glared at her dad and then ran after Noah.

The next two months were what Aspen and Noah described to Krista and Derrick as a living hell.

The two kids were so upset by the news, when they weren't helping their parents pack, they wanted to be with their friends at the beach.

Mom had suggested Aspen spend Spring Break with Krista, maybe stay at her house. Aspen readily agreed and when she did Noah asked if he could stay with Derrick. He met no resistance from their parents.

For Aspen and Krista, the week of surfing, shopping and fun carried with it an underlying dread that once this week ended, Aspen would be moving away and the reality of it often turned the girls to tears.

They reminisced about their crazy adventures together, rehashing things over and over. They poured over pictures, selecting a few special ones with particular meaning. One in particular was the bridge in Orangeville when they visited Krista's great grandma. The bridge held a secret the two of them would probably take to their graves. They laughed when they talked about telling Krista's parents now. But changed their minds almost as quickly.

"That can wait," Krista had concluded. "We can confess later. After all, we have the rest of our lives."

Considering their time was so short, they decided shopping was not a priority and spent most of their waking hours at their beloved beach.

One afternoon, Krista and Derrick surprised Aspen and Noah with a small going away party—but they didn't want it to be too big. Noah was convinced they would be back before school started so why make a fuss about them leaving.

Aspen wished she felt the same conviction he did, but she didn't. And she did not know why.

On the last day of Spring Break the two girls straddled their surfboards waiting for a set. They could see it coming and both readied themselves to jump to their feet, but when they looked directly at each other, they both started to cry and stayed sitting on their boards letting the wave pass them by. They paddled out away from most of the surfers and talked—and cried some more.

During the conversation about anything and everything, Krista's mood took on a serious tone when she said, "Aspen I want you to know something. I don't pretend to understand the—you know, the invisible people, or spirits or whatever they are—I don't know what you are talking about. But I do know this, I trust you. Even since Kindergarten when you had that imaginary…" she stopped when she realized how she had referred to Sami and she caught the discretionary look on Aspen's face.

Aspen smiled but she said nothing.

Krista continued, "you know what I mean."

Aspen nodded.

Krista said, "the thing is, I have no reason not to believe you and I know it has been hard to talk to anyone in your family about it. But I have to tell you Aspen when Great Grandma Minnie had so much confidence in you it really made me think. There is something real to what is going on with you. And then at the bridge—I didn't see anyone but somehow I miraculously got out of the water and I did not do it on my own. Maybe someday I will totally understand but for now, I want you to know that I trust you and believe you. I guess I just needed you to know that."

The girls laid across their boards facing each other. Aspen reached for her best friend's hands and squeezed them. "I have always known that you believe in me, Krista, even if in your heart you questioned my sanity." She chuckled. "You would not be the only one. But I trust you with my life and every secret. You are the sister I have never had and the best friend in the history of the world. I love you, Krista."

She let go of Krista's hands and pulled herself up onto her board, laying on her back.

Krista did the same and they floated in silence for several minutes.

When Krista spoke, she choked on her words, "I...I love you too, Aspen. You are my best friend forever and ever."

Aspen was silent, but then she said almost in a whisper, "I know, and I'm sorry. Cause best friends don't leave."

The girls rolled onto their stomachs and for several seconds stared into each other's tear-stained eyes. Neither spoke, there was nothing let to say.

Minutes later, they caught a perfect wave, rode it all the way in and decided it was an epic way to end the day.

Aspen, Noah and their mom and dad were leaving San Clemente at 5am the next morning—Saturday—a day that she usually looked forward to, but now she dreaded.

Aspen sat up all night, tears flowing freely down her cheeks. The house was silent. Life, as she knew it, seemed to be coming to an end.

Dad drove the truck away from the house and up the winding street. Aspen leaned out of the window waving until Krista's family, Krista, and Derrick, finally disappeared from her view when the truck rounded a corner.

She sank back into her seat and closed her eyes, uncontrollable sobs wrenching her chest.

Her heavy heart nearly consuming her entire being, Aspen could not have known this would be the last time she would see her treasured best friend—at least in her body.

THE END

OTHER BOOKS
BY DEBBIE IHLER RASMUSSEN

Mystic Angel

Mystic Lake

Mystic Mansion

Watch for the next back story…

Sometimes Love Just Isn't

ABOUT THE AUTHOR

Author of *The Mystic Trilogy*, Debbie Ihler Rasmussen takes readers into a world of the paranormal, adventure, and mystery.

Six children, seventeen grandchildren, (who now live in three states) forty-four years of teaching dance, church service, random jobs, adventures, travel, and scores of treasured friends, add to her library of characters and ideas.

Best Friends Don't Leave is the first in a series of back stories that lend to the history of the many interesting, mysterious, and complicated characters in Mystic Trilogy.

Currently Debbie lives in the shadows of the majestic Wasatch Mountains in Salt Lake City, Utah where she loves the spring, summer and fall—and tolerates the winters. She gives thanks to God for her family, her friends, and the blessing of writing. She loves (and misses) the beach, running (recently walking!) cycling, hiking, reading, and fun!